LIZARD LOVE

lizard love

WENDY TOWNSEND

Front Street
Asheville, North Carolina

Library of Congress Cataloging-in-Publication Data
Townsend, Wendy.
Lizard love / Wendy Townsend. — 1st ed.
p. cm.
Summary: Grace, a teenager, and her mother have moved
to Manhattan where she feels alienated and out of place,
far from the ponds and farm where she grew up playing
with bullfrogs and lizards, until she finds Fang & Claw,
a reptile store, and meets the owner's son, Walter.
ISBN 978-1-932425-34-5 (hardcover : alk. paper)
[1. Reptiles—Fiction. 2. Self-acceptance—Fiction.
3. Interpersonal relations—Fiction. 4. City and town
life—New York (State)—New York—Fiction.
5. Country life—Middle West—Fiction. 6. New York
(N.Y.)—Fiction.] I. Title.
PZ7.T6672Li 2008   [Fic]—dc22
2007017975

FRONT STREET
An Imprint of Boyds Mills Press, Inc.
815 Church Street
Honesdale, Pennsylvania 18431

For Spot and all his kin, and for Mark

Prologue

"I have a wedding dress," I told the bullfrog. His legs hung, dripping, down to my elbows. His arms rested on my thumbs, which were wrapped around his belly. I kissed his cool, moist lips. He kept still except for his drumming yellow throat. "It's lace all the way down to my feet. And when I spin around, it goes out!"

The bullfrog blinked one of his big eyes, and I worried that he might be feeling dry. But the coppery sheen on his moss-green back still glistened in the morning sunlight. I looked at the gray and white mottling around his belly and on the undersides of his legs. He pushed against my thumbs with his thumbs and lifted one of his legs, then let it go limp.

"Don't be scared," I said. "I'll let you go now."

He got scared sometimes when I held him, but I knew the bullfrog was my friend, because no matter how many times I caught him, he was always here by the pond. He never went away.

I lowered him into the water and opened my hands. "Bye, Bullfrog," I whispered. He waited only a second, then shot toward deep water, his arms back along his sides. With one scissor kick of his long legs, he disappeared.

I looked back at the pond's edge. Two little cricket frogs sat in the shallow water, their pulsing throats making ripple rings around them. Cricket frogs were the colors of mud: shades of gray and brown, with flecks of rust-red. They sang fast, *click-click-click-click*, while the bullfrog bellowed, *rraalmph-rraalmph*. I knew they were quick, so I crouched and crept closer to them. Suddenly they jumped into the air and came down in deep water.

"You have to sneak up on them," Grandpa said, walking up the dam. "Like this."

Grandpa took small, quiet steps near the pond, his eye on the water's edge. He squatted in the grass. I followed. His arm ready and his blue eyes fixed on a spot in the mud, Grandpa held still as a heron watching a minnow. I held my breath. Then, quick, Grandpa's hand swept down and closed around something. He took my hand and, cupping it under his fist, let the tiny wet frog drop into my palm.

"Hold on to him," Grandpa said, grinning, and headed for the garden. I cupped both my hands around the frog, but he could not be still. He jumped against my fingers like popcorn popping.

When the cricket frog stopped jumping, I opened my hands just a little. I saw his skin, not smooth like the bullfrog's but with bumps all over. I saw his toes, tiny as snail's antennae, and I opened my hands a little more to see his eyes. They were teeny black round pupils set in bronze beads. When I talked to him, the frog sprang through the air in an arc and landed with a *plink* in deep water. But I knew he would come back, and I would catch him the way Grandpa had showed me, and soon the cricket frog would be my friend, too.

Grandpa's tiller started and I ran to the garden. Standing at one end of the giant dirt rectangle I watched Grandpa and Grandma working. Grandma bent over a row of leafy plants, weeding, her baggy shorts flapping around her knees, her sneakers muddy. Grandpa had on his heavy work boots and gray trousers. He guided the tiller across the garden, churning up dark, moist soil. The earth smell was strong, hot-wet like manure in the summer sun. Grandpa swatted at a deer fly that circled his head.

I went over to Grandma. The soft garden soil felt cool and good between my toes. I couldn't understand why Grandpa and Grandma wore shoes all the time—I never wore them if I didn't have to. I never wore anything but my shorts.

"Hi, sweetheart," Grandma shouted over the tiller's motor, not looking up.

"Can I help?" I shouted back. Grandma wrapped her thick fingers around a clump of weeds, twisted it and yanked it out of the ground, threw it down. A drop of sweat hung from her nose.

"Start at the other end," she hollered. "Try to get the whole weed, roots and all."

Crouching at the end of the beet row I started to pull weeds, anything without a red stem. I watched Grandma shake the soil off the weeds' roots and did the same. I wanted to talk about Aunt Marcia's wedding, but Grandpa's tiller was too loud. Trucks had come to the house all week delivering boxes sealed with white tape, and just yesterday a truck came loaded with potted trees and terra cotta statues of fat angels holding birds. A black car came, too, and a man wearing a suit got out and followed Grandma around the house. She pointed at the lilac bushes, the brick wall beside the herb garden, and the ivy bed around the patio. The man in the suit carried a notebook and nodded, and told the truck driver where to put the trees and angel statues.

I felt thirsty, but I hadn't pulled many weeds yet. I kept working. I thought about my wedding dress and how I would wear it and twirl and run through the woods to the pond where my bullfrog lived. But I wouldn't get to wear it until Saturday, for Marcia's wedding.

Mom would come for the wedding. She would drive up from Bloomington. She stayed there during the week, in that old apartment, so she could go to college. But I got to stay in Mooresville for the whole summer because my school was over.

Last Saturday, Grandma took Mom and me to the bridal shop to be fitted in our dresses. My other aunt, Janice, was there, and a woman who had been in college with Marcia. They were the bridesmaids. I was the only flower girl because I was the only grandchild, Grandma said.

I stood in the dressing room with tall women in rustling white dresses around me. I looked up at their bodies all in white, their slender waists, their long hair pinned up on their heads. Above me slim arms reached to fix pearl buttons while the shop lady went around with pins. Then it was my turn.

"Arms in the air," the lady said. She slid the dress down over my head, and I saw bright white, smelled a clean, new smell. The lace brushed my eyelashes on its way down to my toes. My head popped out the other side and in the mirror I saw my brown-skinned, bramble-scratched arms coming out of the white dress, my sun-streaked hair cut short around staring brown eyes. I half-twirled so the lace skirt fluffed out.

"Take a deep breath," the shop lady said. She snugged the waist in at my back and put a pin there. "Okay," she said, "arms up!"

—

Grandpa's tiller hitched and chugged. My legs ached, and I felt sweaty and heavy-headed. Grandma worked fast, getting closer, heaps of weeds behind her. I looked back at my small piles of weeds wilting in the sun. I touched the back of my head. It was hot like the hood of a car in summertime.

The tiller motor stopped. I could hear a robin singing with Grandma's breathy humming. I watched her strong hands, bits of soil flying as she pulled and shook the weeds. Sweat glistened on her face.

"I'm hot," I said.

"Go jump in the pool," Grandma said. I looked over my shoulder at Grandpa hoeing a neat row through the soil he'd tilled. Then I saw the trays of tomato sets. Grandma and Grandpa were going to work all day. They'd stop for lunch and go right back to work afterward, the way they always did. But ever since Marcia's wedding got started, they worked even harder. I stood up and my head swirled. I stepped over the row of peas and started for the pool.

"Don't walk where Grandpa just tilled," Grandma hollered. "You'll compact the soil!"

I tiptoed out of the garden the shortest way.

My bullfrog plopped into the water with a *rrulph* when I ran past. I ran uphill through the woods and out the other side into bright sunshine at the hilltop.

Standing on the ledge that went around the pool, I looked down into the deep end. The water seemed alive. Then I saw the mud ringing my ankles and clotted between my toes.

Grandpa didn't want me to wash my feet in the pool. I was supposed to get the hose. I looked across the wide, hot patio at the hose, then over my shoulder toward the garden beyond the woods. I could see moving patches of white and pale blue, Grandma's and Grandpa's shirts. I took a breath, dove in. Opening my eyes to clear, cool blue, I let my arms float. Mud fell from between my toes. Underwater the gritty sweat and tiredness went away.

Here, I could be fast. I pushed off the wall with my feet and shot through the water like my bullfrog. I saw my shadow pass over the drain at the bottom. I could be slow if I wanted. Bringing my hands together out in front, I turned them into sea turtle flippers and cut back against the water to push ahead and glide.

Grandma had showed me how to do a racing dive, how to stay on top of the water. She'd taught me to swim the crawl, to turn my head to the side and catch a breath every other armstroke and do laps back and forth across the pool. But I didn't practice it. All that movement between air and water— that was for trying to get *across*. I wanted to be *under*.

After lunch I watched Grandma and Grandpa put their muddy shoes back on to go work in the hot afternoon sun. I wanted a Dairy Queen. I wanted Grandpa to be relaxed, driving us into town for ice cream. "Don't we need something from town?"

"No, sweetheart," Grandma said. "Do you need something from town?"

"No, just—" I shook my head. "Nothing."

"Grandpa and I have to get all the tomatoes in this afternoon. You're on your own, okay?"

"Okay." I followed my grandparents to the edge of the patio and watched them walk downhill into the woods.

I wasn't sad. I had my own friends. I could see my bullfrog again, or try to catch a cricket frog. Or I could visit the mice who built a nest in the pump house, or the doves who nested in the spruce trees. I could find the salamanders who lived in the fallen hemlock tree down by the ravine, or the turtles who basked on the willow stump in the pond.

In hot weather my walks began in the pool so I could start out wet. Some days I went one way, climbing out of the pool's deep end and heading down the path my grandparents had just taken through the woods, and some days I went the other way, starting out from the shallow end and heading to the stable in the field. Today the stable would be good. I dropped into the pool and sank, my cheeks puffed out. Blowing bubbles, I pushed off the bottom toward the shallow end.

Wet hair and wet shorts kept me cool as I walked to the stable. Barn swallows had made a mud nest inside like a clay pot built against a ceiling beam. Two days ago I had reached into the nest and felt six paper-fragile eggs the size of jellybeans nestled in a bowl of feathers.

Like a cave in the middle of a field, the cinder-block stable was built into the side of the hill with two wide stalls, one big enough for Grandpa's blue Ford tractor. There had been horses once, but now the stable belonged to mice and birds and spiders.

I stepped across a sharp line between bright sunlight and shadow made by the stable roof. Straining to see the swallow's nest with eyes not used to the dark, I saw no tail feathers, no Mama bird on eggs. Maybe she was out finding food for new babies. In the corner of the stable, shafts of sunlight came through dusty windows framed by dusty spiderwebs. The dust was brown, the color of garden mud. Grandpa's blue Ford sat asleep. It was the only thing without dust on it.

Fluttering wings and a screeching *chee-chee!* startled me—Mama swallow had been on her nest after all. I listened for the soft peeping of babies, but I didn't hear any.

Another fluttering came from a window. A struggling moth, his back legs caught in an old spiderweb, beat his wings against the glass and stirred up little clouds of dust. I went to him. On the sill below lay the stiff, dried bodies of wasps, bumblebees, and moths who hadn't been able to get out. I pinched the live moth's wings shut and carried him to the stable entrance. His six legs kicked wildly. I pulled strands of sticky spider silk from his legs, then opened my fingers and watched his fluttering, bobbing flight toward the woods. I looked at my thumb and finger, at the powdery scales from the moth's wings that were the colors of pearly wood dust.

Mama swallow flew down from her nest screeching *chee-chee! chee-chee!* On her way out she swooped over my head, and I saw her rusty-apricot breast, her pointed black wings and scissor-tail.

I dragged the five-gallon oil drum from Grandpa's tractor over so that I could see the swallows' nest when I climbed on top. Mama returned with Papa swallow, their scolding *chee-chees!* loud inside the stable, making me duck. The birds flew back out. I felt scared because Mama and Papa swallow were angry at me for being too close to their nest. Grandma said people mustn't touch birds' eggs or babies because the parents will abandon the nest. But it wasn't true. I had touched the swallows' eggs, and Mama and Papa came back.

I needed to feel inside the nest, to just pet the babies quick. Up on my tiptoes, holding my breath, I reached up and touched naked warm skin and shell: the eggs were hatching. I let my fingers stay on the trembling baby birds a moment and I breathed.

I pulled my hand away and got down off the oil drum just as Mama and Papa circled inside again, screeching. I pressed against the cinder-block wall to give them space to reach the nest. The swallows would see that I was their friend—I had petted their new babies so gently. I tiptoed out the stable entrance.

Organ music played slow and serious while I walked up the aisle, up the long white sheet that was laid over red church carpet. A ring of daisies rested on my head, and I wore white gloves with pearl buttons at my wrists. On both sides, people sitting in benches made breathy noises when I passed, but I didn't look at them. I was looking down at my tight white shoes, concentrating: *left foot, wait, right foot, wait.* Every right step I gathered rose petals from my basket and sprinkled them on the sheet.

At the end of the sheet I turned and walked in front of the bench where Grandma sat. I glanced at her, then kept walking to the place I was supposed to stand, the way I did in rehearsal. Mom followed me. When she reached the end of the sheet, she turned and pranced toward me in her white bridesmaid's dress. Her lips were tight and I knew she was trying not to giggle. Mom was always being silly, especially when it wasn't time to be. Aunt Janice came next, looking like Mom's twin, only her face was serious, her walk in perfect time with the organ music. Marcia's college friend followed and stood beside Janice; then we watched Marcia and Grandpa walk up the aisle to where Larry and the minister waited.

Grandpa looked extra-clean, his face tight and serious. His suit was so black, his hair cut so short I could see the skin on his head. Marcia looked like a queen. She wore white gloves that went up her arms past her elbows. Her dress was long and white and clung to her legs and hips and body. Down the front, pearl and crystal beads swirled in a pattern of vines and leaves. Her bouquet had a trailing chain of roses and ferns that almost reached the ground. Her face looked beautiful, but then I saw that her eyes were red and teary. I reached up to find my mother's hand, and through our white gloves our fingers clasped.

"Why is Marcia sad?" I asked Mom, tugging on her hand. But the organ music was loud and she shook her head to say she couldn't hear me.

When Grandpa and Marcia came to the end of the aisle the organ stopped and the minister started talking. Marcia's veil covered the side of her face. I looked up at the high church ceiling where the minister's voice echoed. My shoes began to hurt. I shifted from one foot to the other and Mom squeezed my fingers. I squeezed back twice. She squeezed three times, I squeezed back four.

Around the altar, giant bouquets of ivory-white flowers and long fern fronds stood in vases as tall as me. The ferns were the same as the ones that grew by the ravine in Mooresville. I wished I was walking through their feathery green leaves in my bare feet, my wedding dress swishing around my ankles.

All of a sudden, loud clapping echoed inside the church and Marcia and Larry kissed. Then the organ played fast, happy music and Marcia didn't look sad anymore, and I was glad because we could all go back to Mooresville and I could take my shoes off.

I stood at the end of the diving board in my bare feet, bouncing to make my dress fluff and wanting to jump in. But two swans made out of white flowers floated in the pool, and I wasn't supposed to make any waves. Four ladies wearing hats and bright-colored dresses stepped out of the porch onto the patio. Guests were arriving, walking up the brick path that came around the herb garden. But I didn't see Marcia. I wished she would hurry up because I wanted to take her down to the pond and show her my bullfrog.

From the diving board I saw how decorated everything was. Huge clay pots with funny trees—their leaves were in a puffy ball at the top—lined the pool's edges, a blue bow tied to each trunk. Round tables dotted the patio, each with four white chairs and a blue tablecloth, each tablecloth with little white pom-poms sewn around the hem. In the center of each table was a candle inside a glass, and a little bouquet of white roses and fern leaves.

The piano had been moved outside while we were at the church. A woman wearing a blue dress with see-through sleeves sat down on the bench, and a man in a white suit stood beside her holding a shiny gold saxophone. When they started to play, the music sounded like Grandma's humming and wind chimes in the breeze. I gathered my skirts and stepped down from the diving board to go watch.

Near the piano stood a table where a man dressed in a black tuxedo poured fizzy golden champagne into rows of crystal glasses. More and more people arrived and took glasses, and the man kept pouring. A camera flashed.

I heard Marcia's voice and followed it, squeezing between the clusters of chattering guests.

"Marcia!" I called out. "Come see my bullfrog!"

"Oh, I want to," she said, bending at her slim white waist. "But I need to be here with our guests." She stroked my hair and it felt good, but then two ladies wearing flowery hats came over and started talking to her and she took her hand away. I gave the ladies what Grandma called my black storm cloud look, but they just smiled. Right then, a white flash made me blink. A man had taken our picture. I went inside to look for my mother.

Guests were all around in the living room and standing by

the fireplace. Instead of a fire burning, there were white roses and fern leaves piled up inside and spilling onto the floor. I found my mother, talking to a man in a blue suit. They each held a glass of champagne. "Mom." I tugged on her dress. "Come see my bullfrog. Please?"

She laughed and put her hand on the back of my neck. "My daughter," she told the man. I looked up at her, waiting. "Maybe later, darling." She patted my back and sipped her champagne. I felt like giving Mom my black storm cloud look. Then I saw Grandpa in his black suit and went over to him. He was holding a champagne glass, too, and talking to a man.

Grandpa put his big hand on my shoulder, hugged me to him. "This is my little granddaughter, Grace," he told the man. "Grace, this is Jack," Grandpa said, gesturing with his glass.

Jack bent his knees, tilted his head. "And how old are you, young lady?"

"Six and a half," I said. "Do you want to see my bullfrog?"

"I'd *love* to meet your frog. Where does he live?"

"Down there." I pointed at the window, toward the pond.

"Sweetheart," Grandpa said, "Jack doesn't want to walk down there in the mud right now."

Jack smiled. "Maybe some other time?"

"I'll go get him," I said. Grandpa patted my arm and said something to Jack about an office. I slipped from under his hand and went outside.

Then I saw the wedding cake. Sitting in the middle of a glass table, it was really four cakes, each with real flowers on top. The cakes got smaller as they went up and had tiny white pillars between them, like the ones in front of the Indianapolis Bank. I put my fingers on the edge of the table, stood on my tiptoes, and leaned closer. The vanilla-smelling frosting looked thick and fluffy, like my dress, but I didn't dare break the swirling patterns with my finger. On the very top, on the smallest layer, sat two china angels, a boy and a girl. Both had short curly hair, but the boy had a cloth that only went around his bottom, and the girl's cloth covered her whole body. Beside the cake a silver knife with a white satin ribbon tied around the handle rested on a bed of fern leaves.

"Hello, flower girl." It was the man with the camera again. "How about a smile?"

I hated being told to smile. But I liked having my picture taken in my dress, and I held the skirt out a little.

A salty, thick odor of roast beef swirled around me. I turned to see the cook bringing out a big roast on a silver platter.

"Let's eat!" Grandpa said.

I had my dinner almost before anyone else because people in the buffet line kept putting me in front of them. At Marcia's table, where I sat, white roses lay piled and scattered around. There were four silver candleholders, each with a porcelain angel clinging to its base and six tall white candles with soft flames at the top.

Daylight was leaving, but the candles made a warm light that wrapped around everything. My belly full, I sat looking at the flowers and ferns that seemed to grow everywhere, at the sparkling crystal and glistening silver, the white satin ribbons and lace. I listened to the grownups laughing, the almost sad humming of the saxophone. I smelled Grandma's peonies, blooming fat pink and white puffs beside the herb garden. I wanted to see my bullfrog.

More champagne corks popped. The camera flashed as Marcia and Larry cut the wedding cake. I took a slice of cake and sat in the corner under a tall candlestick holder that was like a pitchfork. The cake tasted like butter and lemon; the frosting was smooth and vanilla-sweet. I licked it from my fingers, licked it from the plate, picked the crumbs from the puffs of my dress.

I looked up and saw Marcia going inside with everyone following, too. The crowd filled the living room and pushed the bridesmaids toward the bottom of the staircase. Marcia stood at the top.

I found Grandma and took her hand. "What's Marcia doing?"

"She's going to throw the bouquet," Grandma said. "Whoever catches it will be the next bride."

I wanted Mom to catch the bouquet, but Aunt Janice caught it. Mom giggled. Marcia's college friend said, "I'm engaged."

And now it was time to get my bullfrog. I started to go. Then a horn honked out by the driveway and I knew it was about Marcia, so I ran out there. People were waving and shouting.

I saw Marcia in the car beside Larry. Her wedding dress was gone and she wore a plain blouse instead. She waved back at the crowd. Her white gloves were gone, too.

"Mom!" I yelled. "Where's Marcia's wedding dress? Where is she going?"

"On her honeymoon!" Mom said, laughing.

Then I knew why Marcia had been sad in the church—because she had to leave Mooresville. I watched Marcia's car go out of the driveway with parked cars on both sides. At the end of the driveway red taillights flashed like monster eyes, and the car disappeared.

Piano music started, and another champagne cork popped. I stood in the driveway feeling the day's heat rising from the pavement. A warm breeze carried the smells of moss and woods. Crickets and cricket frogs began to chirp and click. A lightning bug flashed. My bullfrog called me, *rraalmph! rraalmph! rraalmph!*

I hurried across the lawn. Dew on the grass wetted the lace hem of my dress around my ankles, cooling, awakening. I looked up into the woods ahead, the trees tall and thick like giant creatures, their soft, leafy arms reaching out to hug me. The trees were huge, especially now, at dusk, when they looked deepest green and shadowy. But it was a welcoming shadowy, and I went into them. Cradled by the humid air around me and the tree giants' arms overhead, I skipped down the packed mud path into the woods, barely able to see the tree roots, but it didn't matter—I knew them all by heart. In the woods it was night already, but on the other side, at the pond, the last daylight still held and the lightning bugs flickered like tiny candle flames scattered through the air.

Cricket frogs quieted and some of them went *plink* into the water as I walked up the dam to my bullfrog's place. As if on cue, he plopped into the water. I followed him into the mud, the water lifting my dress so that it billowed. The water and mud felt warm near the pond's edge, cooler as I stepped deeper, reached down under to where my bullfrog hid. In the loose, silken mud I felt his slippery sides and closed my fingers around his belly as he gave a half-kick. I lifted him out of the water, brought him to me, hugged him gently. He wriggled and drew his legs under himself so that he was sitting on my chest.

Clinging to my bullfrog I listened to the cricket frogs begin to sing again, one voice, then two more, until many *click-click-clicked* around us, filling the twilight air. Two nighthawks, calling *peeert, peeert,* flew overhead. Thick with moisture, the air made foggy rings around each lightning bug and around the moon, which peeked over the treetops. Through the trees I could just see patches of light from the house. I felt my bullfrog's cool wetness seeping through my dress to my skin, but he would not dry out because the sun was down and it was frog-time.

"See my wedding dress?" I said. And I kissed his damp lips.

New York City

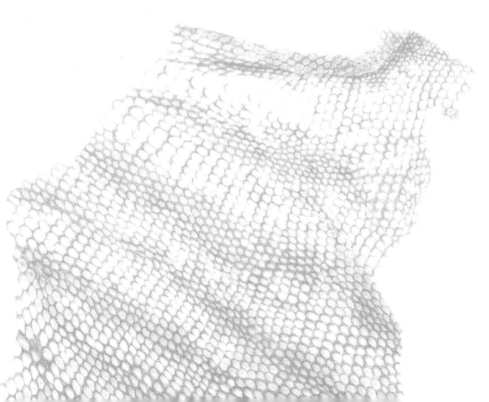

I found Fang & Claw by accident. I was riding the subway home from school, crammed against the pole by people in heavy coats. Every time the train lurched into a station I gripped the pole hard and tried not to bump into anyone. I looked at the tired faces and wondered, why are all these people here? Did someone make them be here? The air had a stuffy, hot smell and there wasn't enough of it. But outside the air was so thin and cold it hurt to breathe, and it stank of exhaust. There was frozen concrete everywhere and everything was gray. I didn't know which was worse, the bitter cold or the stifling heat of late summer, when my mother made us move here.

A sticky-looking spill spread slowly on the floor and I was trying not to step in it. I shut my eyes and wished hard that I could be back in Mooresville, where winter was so quiet on some days I could hear only snow falling on dry beech leaves and smell only wood smoke from the fireplace. The train jerked to a stop and the doors rattled open.

I looked up in time to see them shut on my stop and I said, "Wait!"

A lady in a fur coat gave me a sour look. Outside the windows the black-and-white-tiled SPRING STREET signs started going by faster and faster until the train roared into the tunnel. I touched the bullfrog I'd painted on my jacket.

My mother had told me what to do if I ever missed my stop. She said to get off at the very next stop, take the overpass across the tracks, and get on the train heading back. The train kept speeding through the tunnel until it finally pulled into a station and slowed and then stopped. The doors opened and I squeezed through the crowd and got out. I didn't want to get on another train, so I climbed out of the station.

It was only three thirty and already the light was fading. People wrapped in dark, thick coats and hats hurried by as I stood on the corner. Cold wind burned my face, and I pulled my jacket close around me. It was a Levi's jacket my mom wore in high school, faded and big enough to wear a heavy sweatshirt underneath. I'd started painting frogs and snakes on it.

I looked across the street and saw a funny building, like a black box stuck between two tall gray ones. It had a sign that said FANG & CLAW, and the letters looked like someone had cut them out of paper with scissors. When the light changed I crossed the street to go see.

Under the FANG & CLAW sign was a window painted black from the inside, so that all I could see was my reflection. An iron gate blocked the entry partway, but through the window in the door I saw a boy holding a long speckled snake. I squeezed by the gate and the boy looked up. I put my hand on the glass. He waved for me to come in, so I did. It was like stepping into a warm summer day. I shut the door quickly behind me. The air smelled like rain soaking the bark Grandma put around her roses.

"Hi," said the boy. He was chubby, with soft-looking skin almost as white as the T-shirt he wore. Across the front it said BRONX ZOO REPTILE HOUSE. His shaggy hair was a pale color. He made me think of the tree frog who blends in with silvery lichen on tree trunks.

"Hi," I said. "Can I hold the snake?"

"Sure."

I held out my hand and let the snake flick my fingers with his tongue, which was red with a black band in the middle. He moved onto my hand, his tongue flicking light as a daddy longlegs walking, his belly scales shifting as he pulled his body across my skin.

"I think he likes you," the boy said. "His name's Pete. He's a pine snake. I'm Walter."

"I'm Grace."

"That's a cool jacket. Nice bullfrog."

"Thanks." Pete's rope-thick coils were filling my hands. "I never held a snake like this before. But one time I caught a black snake in the stable. That was at my grandma and grandpa's house, where my bullfrog lives."

Walter let go of Pete's tail. "You miss your bullfrog?"

A man poked his head out from behind a curtain and looked over the tops of his glasses. "Hello, young lady."

I said hi and smiled. He looked like a mad scientist, with his thick white mustache and wild hair.

"That's my dad," Walter said. "Everyone calls him Pops."

Pops held up a snake as long as Pete but a lot thicker. "This is Sue. Can you give me a hand, Walt?"

"'Scuse me," Walter said to me. Before he disappeared behind the curtain, I saw a giant pair of tweezers sticking out of his back pocket and wondered what they were for.

Pete slid through my hands, weaving between my fingers. His skin felt smooth and rough at the same time, like the wooden handle of my grandpa's old hoe. He didn't blink; he had no eyelids. But his eyes moved under clear eye caps as he started to climb up my arm. I rested my cheek against his scaly back.

I looked at the tanks and wooden boxes on the shelves that reached from floor to ceiling all the way around the room. The boxes had windows, and the ones higher up had red lights inside. Some were big enough for me to lie down in. Way at the top I saw the glossy white throat of a snake rise behind the glass. His head was bigger than my fist. I could hear Walter talking to his dad. Both of them had a New York accent. How could someone be from here and know about snakes?

A sound like water bubbling came from behind, and I turned around. A snapping turtle big as a frying pan stood in a tank full of water so clear that I could see every detail, as if he were behind a magnifying glass. He was stretching his long neck up to the water's surface, and I could see his perfectly round eyes and the sharp edges of his jaws. He had thick, wrinkly legs and webbed feet and a long stegosaurus tail. His bumps and spiky bits of skin all over made him look even more like a dinosaur turtle than the snappers I knew.

Walter came back. "That's a special snapper," I said.

"Yep. An alligator snapper from down south." Walter put his hand on the glass and watched the turtle. Light from the water made his gray eyes silver. "The alligator snapper grows a lot larger than the common snapper. But he's really shy. You can't keep them together or they fight and the common snapper wins."

"When I used to find snappers in Grandpa's pond I'd pull the leeches off their bottoms."

"Your grandparents' place sounds great. How come you're in the city now?"

"My mother goes to school here."

"Oh." Walter touched Pete's tail, curled around my hand. "Hey, do you want to see an iguana? I raised him from a baby."

I nodded. Walter helped me get Pete unwound from my arm and settled down inside his tank. I hung up my jacket on a hook on the wall, next to a coat that must have been Walter's, and followed him behind the curtain.

Pops stood beside a deep metal sink with the snake named Sue draped around his neck, studying something on her head. I looked around the room. Tall shelves against one wall were stacked with rows of plastic boxes. Inside the boxes white rats and mice rattled water bottles and chewed on biscuits. There was a tank busy with crickets—not black, like the Mooresville kind, but sand-colored—chirping and crawling on paper egg cartons. In the opposite wall was a door with a sign that said DO NOT FEED THE ALLIGATORS.

"He's up top, Walt." Pops smiled at me and went back to examining Sue's head.

"There, on top of the cage," Walter said, pointing.

I looked up into the dark gold eye of a big lizard, calmly looking back at me. I caught my breath: he was the most wonderful creature I could ever imagine. He had a great spiky crest and a black-banded tail hanging down. The scales around his head looked like jewels of all different sizes and shades of green, turquoise, and bronze. One of his feet hung down, and each long toe had a curved claw at the tip.

"I call him Spot," Walter said. "Like the dragon the boy keeps under the stairs in that old TV show?"

I hadn't seen the show, but it didn't matter. "Where is he from?"

"A couple of years ago he came in with a bunch of hatchlings from Ecuador. He was really sick and the others climbed all over him like he didn't exist. I set him up back here in his own tank. Within a year he outgrew it and we built this cage. He's never actually *in* it, though. I wish I had more time with him."

"If he were mine, I'd be with him all the time."

"You can hold him."

I held up my hands. Spot's eyelid changed shape, first squinting, then opening up, and his round, oil-black pupil focused. He flicked my finger with his tongue. It was fat and pink, with just the tip forked. I slid my hands underneath his body and took him in my arms. I loved that he was big enough to hold on to and the way his claws gripped my shoulder. His tail went down past my waist. He flicked my cheek with his tongue and I put my face closer to his and breathed in. He had a smell that was like salt and beeswax and something else I couldn't name, yet it was familiar.

A frog called out in the other room. He made a ringing sound, like when you run a wet finger around the rim of a glass.

"There goes Henry," Walter said. "Always at sunset, even though he can't see it."

I held on tight to Spot. His claws dug into my sweatshirt. "I'm supposed to be home by dark. How much is he?"

"Oh, he's not for sale."

I lowered my eyes, ashamed for asking, and started to unhook his claws from my sweatshirt. "Thanks for letting me hold him."

As Walter took Spot away I watched him claw the air and blink his golden eyes. I still had hold of his tail.

"Why don't you come visit?" Walter said.

"Tomorrow?"

"We're closed weekends. If you come back Monday I'll wait for you to feed him."

"Okay." I let go of Spot's tail.

When I got home my mother's schoolbooks and papers were spread out on the table with the week's mail. She stood at the stove stirring a pot of chili while her cat, Freda, sat close by. Mom's blond braid hung down her back. I dropped my jacket on a chair and leaned against her and took the long braid in my hand.

"On the train home I missed my stop, but I found a special place."

"You did? Tell me." She took off her glasses and set them on a book that lay open on the counter.

"It's a pet shop where they have only reptiles. And frogs. And they have an iguana named Spot."

"Spot the iguana?"

"He looks like a spiky dragon with golden eyes and he's this big." I held my hands apart to show her. "Walter let me hold him."

"That was nice of him." She patted my behind. "How about setting the table."

I took silverware and napkins and cups over and stood looking at the mess. The building shook as another truck hit the potholes in the street outside. Our apartment was on a truck route through lower Manhattan.

"Mom? When I held Spot I was happy. He let me hold him close and he kept still, like he was happy too. Not like Freda—she's always struggling to get away whenever I try to hold her. "

"That's just how cats are. So independent, you know? Shove those papers aside, honey."

"I know, Mom. Anyway, I really, really wish I had Spot."

She brought two bowls of chili to the table. "How do you take care of an iguana?"

"It's easy. I mean, he's got a big cage, but he's always sitting on top—that's how tame he is. And he eats only green leaves and fruit. You'd really like him."

"I'm sure I would."

We sat down to eat, and right away Freda jumped into Mom's lap. I didn't think that cat was so independent, not when it came to my mother.

"Mom?"

"How much is he?"

The heater that hung from the ceiling came on. It looked like a dirty old car engine and it ran all the time, blasting hot air across the room. I mashed beans against the side of the bowl with my spoon. "He's not for sale."

"That's too bad. Maybe there's another lizard you want."

"No, I want Spot."

She sighed as though she was very tired. "I know you do."

"Walter said I could visit."

"Well, there you are. You can go play with Spot."

"But it's not the same! I want him here with me."

"Grace, you're whining. I wish I could help, but if Spot isn't for sale, what can I do?"

She pushed aside her bowl and pulled the papers closer again. Freda squinted at me with her yellowy-green eyes. I stacked the dishes and carried them to the sink.

"Just leave them, honey. Thanks."

"Mom?"

She looked up at me. Her reading glasses made her blue eyes enormous.

I didn't want us to be angry at each other. We'd done that back in September, when we were unpacking. It was so hot the dirt stuck to my skin. My head ached, and all I could think about was being under water in Grandma and Grandpa's pool.

"Why did we have to leave Mooresville?" I'd asked.

Mom hadn't answered. She kept taking dishes out of a box and wadding up the newspapers they were wrapped in.

Sitting on her mattress on the floor, I started taking books out of a box one at a time. I remembered how Marcia had cried at her wedding because she was leaving Mooresville. After that I swore I'd never get married. But then my mother had tried to move us away. She took us to Colorado, where she was

going to be a teacher. We lived in a dirty apartment that she couldn't get the bad smell out of. There were cracks in everything, and brown carpet and brown furniture, and her bed came out of the wall.

"I bet we'll go home," I said, "same as we did the first time we left."

My mother stopped unpacking. She turned around and looked at me hard. "You could go to your room."

I had done that—I'd gone to my room—because I was mad, and whenever we were mad at each other I felt so alone my heart thumped with fear and I didn't know what to do.

Now my mother sat at the table, still waiting. "Grace?" she said. "Was there something you wanted to ask?"

"Never mind."

I took my jacket to my room and shut the door. I swept the bottles of fabric paint off my desk into the box and took it up the ladder to my bed. Then I kicked off my sneakers and let them drop to the floor.

Sitting cross-legged, I put my jacket down in front of me and turned on the light. I wanted Spot right there, right on the sleeve, holding on to my shoulder, with his tail going all the way down my arm. I took the cap off the black pen and sketched a long, flat triangle for his head. For his spine and tail I drew a line from the triangle down the sleeve to the cuff. Four lines bent at the elbows and knees made arms and legs, with lines at the ends for fingers and toes. Then I gave the lines shape, fleshing out ribs, belly, and arm and leg muscles. I gave each finger and toe a curved claw. Finally I shaped his head

and the flap of skin at his throat that Walter said was a dewlap. Then I drew his eye, looking out.

I put the cap back on the pen and studied my drawing. The black lines were sketchy and flat on the faded denim, but even so, he looked like Spot.

It was too late to start painting, but at least I could pick out the colors. I turned the box upside down and dumped the bottles of paint on my bed, then spread them out. His body and legs would be olive-green and gray. I chose some blues, oranges, yellow ochre, several shades of green and bronze and copper. I needed black for his eye and the stripes on his tail. I lined up the paints beside my bed and put the rest back in the box.

Even with the lights out, my room was never really dark, because of the streetlamp outside the window. I looked at the pictures of dinosaurs and reptiles I had cut out of *National Geographic* magazines and pinned to the wall. My favorite was a foldout of a swamp that I had pinned to the ceiling. It was dusk in the picture. I lay on my back and looked at the lightning bugs that glowed in the moist air. Enough moonlight reflected on the water to see how thick and leafy the forest was. There would be turtles swimming under the water and frogs calling to each other from where they were perched on cattails and water lilies. I could almost feel the soft mud between my toes and smell the mossy warm earth.

Outside, snow began to fall. I wondered what Spot was doing, whether he was sound asleep, or awake and feeling alone. At least he had frogs and crickets to sing to him. I looked at the bottles of paint lined up for the morning. I wanted to finish painting Spot before Cathy came to get me.

The first time I saw Cathy was on the subway platform. It was after Christmas vacation, and I had just started at my new school. I stood there waiting for the train when this tall blond girl with red velvet patches on her jeans came toward me. She wore clogs, and the wooden *clop* of her footsteps echoed in the tunnel.

"Hey," she said, "you're new at Friends." She gave my jacket a nod. "You paint the frog?"

"Yeah."

"It's nice."

"Thanks." I turned to look down the subway tunnel, but I didn't see any headlights. The girl stood there. I decided to say something. "They're slow today."

"Maybe the tracks are frozen." She put her hands in her coat pockets. "Anyway, I'm Cathy. I live over on the Bowery. In a loft. My dad's an artist."

"I'm Grace."

"You live near here?"

"Spring Street."

"God, you're practically around the corner from me. You live in a loft too?"

"I have a loft bed."

"What grade are you in?"

"Eighth."

"I'm a freshman. Where'd you transfer from?"

"P.S. 130. I got punched in the nose, so my mom took me out of there."

"No kidding. What did you do?"

"The girl said I was looking at her."

"Were you?"

"I guess. I don't know."

"You gotta watch out around here. Some kids will kick your butt just for fun. Especially if you're different."

"Different?"

"Well, let's see. You're walking around in a jacket with snakes and frogs painted all over. But you're not so tough, are you?"

"Why do you say that?"

"Because you're gripping that big frog on your jacket like a kid holding on to a stuffed animal."

We looked at each other and she smiled.

"Here comes our train," she said.

When the door buzzer sounded that Saturday morning I knew it was Cathy. I knew she'd have her dog, Nitely, with her and that she'd want us to go walking around the city. I wanted to finish painting Spot, but my mother would make me go, I knew it. She was thrilled that I had a friend. She buzzed Cathy in and I sat there with a bottle of paint in my hand, listening to clogs clopping up the stairs and Nitely's leash jingling. The moment the door opened there was a scramble of cat and dog toenails scraping the floor and leash chain yanking and Cathy yelling, "Nitely!"

"Oh, never mind the cat," my mother said. "Grace is in her room. Go right in."

I looked at my painting and how the greens and golds and blues glistened in the light. It was the best time of day, when sunlight filled my room. I jammed the cap back on the bottle of green and threw it in the box.

Cathy climbed up and sat down on the top step. I could smell winter on her coat.

"Hi. What're you doing?"

"Painting my jacket."

"Looks like some kind of dragon."

"He's Spot. A lizard I want."

Nitely whined. "Hush, Nitely," Cathy said. "What do you do with a lizard?"

"Same thing you do with Nitely."

"Can you walk a lizard?"

"No!"

"I was kidding, Grace. I'm sure your lizard is totally cool. Anyway, let's go outside. The snow is melting already."

"I can't. My jacket's wet."

"Don't be ridiculous," my mom said, from the other room. "Put on that nice wool coat your grandmother bought. You haven't worn it once."

Cathy grinned. "Come on, you."

I climbed down after Cathy. Nitely wagged his tail, whacking the ladder so hard it had to hurt. He could not stop wiggling and prancing around. His nails clicked the floor and his leash jingled. It made me edgy. The fur around his ankles was wet from the snow and he smelled musky. When Cathy knelt and ruffed Nitely's fur he licked her right on the mouth. I winced and turned away to get the coat from the back of my closet.

Nitely kept shoving his nose in my face while I tried to put on my boots. I shut my eyes and pressed my lips together.

Cathy said, "Stop it, Nitely." He didn't pay any attention.

The sidewalks were wet from melting snow. Salt crystals crunched under our shoes, and the scraping of shovels against concrete echoed up and down side streets. The air was cold, but when we turned up Broadway and walked in the sun we had to unbutton our coats. Nitely trotted beside Cathy with his head down, sniffing everything. My stomach rolled every time he touched his nose to something really disgusting.

Cathy tugged on the leash and said, "Heel."

People hurried by and cars and buses and taxicabs came speeding down the street, horns honking. A fire engine roared around the corner with the siren screaming and red lights flashing. I covered my ears and shut my eyes. I felt Cathy's hand on my arm.

When the fire engine had gone by, Cathy let go of my arm. "You've been here a while, Grace. Why aren't you used to it?"

I put my hands in my coat pockets. I didn't answer, I just walked along, watching the sidewalk, waiting for my heartbeat to slow back down.

"There *are* some great things about the city, you know. Like Ray's Pizza. It's up ahead a few blocks and I'm starved."

Outside the pizza place Cathy tied Nitely's leash to a parking meter. "Stay," she said.

He sat and looked at her and whined and swept the sidewalk with his tail.

Behind the counter a man in a white apron was cutting pizza with a rolling blade.

"Two slices," Cathy told him. "And two sodas."

We took our food to a narrow counter by the window, and Cathy waved at Nitely. He wagged his tail. Cathy shook red pepper flakes all over her pizza, so I did the same to mine.

"I was in the woods once," she said. "On a school trip in the fourth grade. We went on a nature walk and learned the names of trees and birds. Then we built a fire and roasted hot dogs and marshmallows."

I looked at Cathy's pink nail polish and had a hard time imagining her stepping over tree roots and walking through mud, especially in those clogs of hers. But it was more than that; it was the way she walked down the street. She never looked at the ground. She walked like she didn't need to look where she was going.

"It's funny," she said. "The way you are here? I was like that in the woods. Every noise made me jump. I was convinced that a bear was going to leap out of the bushes and that rattlesnakes were behind every stone and log."

She tore the paper off a straw, jammed it into her soda, and took a drink. "Anyway, let's go. I need some things from the drugstore."

The drugstore was across the street. Cathy tied Nitely up again, this time to a street sign.

"Doesn't he get cold?"

"Nah, he's got a nice thick coat. Don't you, boy?" She ruffed his fur and he licked her face.

Cathy took a shopping basket and walked up and down the aisles, plucking things off shelves—barrettes, purple soap, cherry cough drops. She found the aisle of nail polish and selected a bottle.

"Pink is great for blonds." Then she looked at me. "For you, red."

She ran her finger across the bottles on the shelf and stopped on a red the color of blood. "Dragon red. Perfect," she said, dropping the bottle in her basket.

"I don't wear nail polish."

"We'll do your toes to start."

I followed Cathy, watching her find all these things she wanted. She was having fun.

"Ooh—rhinestone earrings." She picked a pair that looked like pink chandeliers off the rack. "Well?" The dangly parts fell to her shoulders as she held the earrings up to her face.

"Nice," I said. A bit of green caught my eye at the end of the aisle. "I'll be right back."

On a shelf between the teddy bears sat a furry stuffed frog. He had a broad smile, wiggly eyes, and floppy legs with webbed feet. I picked him up and pressed him against my face. He smelled like polyester.

"Those are for little kids," Cathy said. "I found you *earrings*." She held up a pair that looked like giant square rubies. "Let me have that." She put the frog back on the shelf and gave me the earrings.

"I can't wear these."

"Why not? Oh, you don't have holes. Well, don't look so miserable—pierced ears are easy to get and it doesn't hurt the way they say it does."

"I'm just tired."

"Okay, we'll go." She picked up a Hershey bar, tossed it in the basket, and headed for the cash register.

Outside, it was getting cold. We buttoned our coats. The sun had gone behind the buildings already, and everything had turned a dim gray. Nitely trotted beside Cathy; his breath came out in steamy puffs. Cathy unwrapped the Hershey bar.

"I want to show you the park." She broke off a piece of chocolate and gave it to me.

We went down Houston Street and then turned onto a quiet block, one that was more like a neighborhood, with low buildings. Some of the windows had flower boxes with brown shriveled leaves hanging down. When Cathy saw another dog on a leash up the block she said, "Let's cross over."

Nitely growled and pulled on the leash, and I could see the other dog doing the same.

Cathy patted Nitely and said, "Good boy."

She was happy, walking along with her dog and her bag of stuff from the drugstore. Nothing bothered her—not the cold, gray everything or the fact that we were walking on concrete with concrete on all sides and ahead as far as we could see.

Finally she stopped. "Here it is," she said. "We'll play handball when it warms up."

Nitely wagged his tail.

I looked at the empty lot Cathy called a park, with buildings on two sides and a tall fence going around the other two.
Beside the fence six bare sycamore trees grew out of squares
of dirt in the sidewalk. The pale branches looked like bones
against the gray sky.

"It looks like a cage."

Cathy sighed, wadded the Hershey bar wrapper, and threw
it into a trash basket. "So, what do *you* want to do?"

"Go home and finish painting my jacket."

We walked.

Cathy said, "Girl, you can't just live in your room. Don't you
want to see the city? There must be something you want to do.
What did you do before you moved here?"

"I played with frogs and turtles at the pond."

"Okay, that's summer. What about winter? You did go to
school, right? Didn't you do stuff with friends, like go to movies?
I know they have huge shopping malls in the Midwest."

"Yeah, I went to school. Then I went straight home and out
in the woods to follow the creek. I'd look at crystal ice patterns
with water running underneath and I'd listen to chickadees
chattering and flitting around in the trees."

"That's beautiful, Grace. But you're here now."

"Yeah, and I hate it."

Then I saw a window that was all green with leaves. It was
right across the street, between a deli and a dry cleaner's. I
crossed and stood in front of the glass. It was like looking into
a giant terrarium, all steamy inside. Palm trees and giant ferns
grew out of pots big as barrels. There were plants I'd never

seen before. Thick, twisted branches hung from the ceiling clustered with plants that looked like silvery spiders. Leafy vines spilled out of pots mounted on the walls so that every inch of space had something growing. The green made my eyes feel better.

"It's closed on weekends," Cathy said. She was looking at a sign on the door.

"Huh?"

"It's *closed*."

I could watch the kids at Friends School without getting punched in the face. The girls in eighth grade wore the same clothes: plaid flannel shirts, faded jeans, hiking boots. They looked like the eighth-grade boys except for their hair and jewelry. The girls put up their hair with clips or pulled it back in a ponytail and wore silver bracelets and rings and heart-shaped earrings made out of pink glass. During free periods the girls sat around in the hall near the lockers, cross-legged, knees touching, closing a circle. They passed around pens and papers and shared granola bars and laughed.

The first Monday that I wore my jacket with Spot painted on the sleeve, instead of hurrying away from my locker I rear-ranged my books, stacking them neatly. The girls sat in their circle. I went over to look at the bulletin board on the wall right across from where they were sitting. I read the volleyball team's game schedule and all the Help Wanted ads. I studied the drama club announcement for the spring play.

Finally I walked away. I felt like an idiot for standing there in my lizard jacket. What did I think—that those girls would speak to me? That one of them might ask about the lizard? Should I have said, *Hi, I'm Grace and this is Spot?* How incredibly dumb.

Later I went to the cafeteria. Since Cathy was in the upper school we had lunch at different times. I opened my biology book and started reading while I ate a peanut butter sandwich. Behind me the eighth graders were having lunch. They started getting loud, crushing soda cans and slurping their drinks through straws. A wadded paper napkin flew over my head and rolled across the table. I shifted my jacket around my shoulders and kept reading about locomotion in single-cell organisms. Someone said, "Lizard," and I turned around. The boys cracked up laughing.

"Hey, Lizard Girl!" one said.

The girls smiled at each other.

That afternoon I sat in math class, watching the clock. The second hand passed the three, and I pulled my backpack strap onto my shoulder and scooted my chair out a little. I hated the way the teacher always held us five extra minutes to squeeze in one more equation. The instant he shut his book, I shut mine, jumped up, and headed for the door. Other kids were already clustered at the lockers when I hurried past.

Someone yelled, "Run, Lizard Girl!"

I wanted to say something smart right back, but I couldn't think. I pushed open the stairwell door and ran down the stairs.

When I climbed out of the Fourteenth Street station it was

getting colder and the light was fading. I couldn't wait to be in the warmth of Fang & Claw. I hurried across the street, holding my collar against the icy wind.

The gate screeched when I pushed it aside, and through the window I could see Walter look up. He held a turtle in one hand. I opened the door and went inside. The turtle stretched out her neck and flapped her webbed hands and feet in the air, flinging drops of water. I rubbed my arms. The paint on my sleeve felt like cold plastic.

"Hey, you painted Spot." Walter put the turtle back in the water and wiped his hands on his T-shirt. "Can I see?"

I turned sideways and held my arm out straight to show him.

Walter ran his finger down the crest of spines and a smile spread across his face. "You got the scales to look real. And his eye—that's just the way he looks when he's happy."

"Thanks. Can I see him?"

"Yeah. He had lunch with the red foots, but I saved his pear for you."

Walter pulled the curtain aside and Pops came out. He had a snake around his neck, a long, slender one this time, with skin like burnished steel.

"Hello, Grace," he said.

"Hi, Pops." I hung up my jacket and went into the back room.

When I saw Spot my chest ached and my throat closed up. He remembered me; I knew it because of the way his eyes focused on mine. I reached up and put my hands on him. He leaned into me and peered over the tops of my fingers to see what Walter was doing.

"He wants his pear," I said.

As soon as Walter put the dish on the counter Spot climbed onto my shoulder. I took half the pear and held it for him while he ate. Juice dripped down his chin onto my wrist. When that was gone I held out my arm so he could climb down and eat the rest himself.

Walter turned on the faucet and washed his hands. I rinsed my hand and took the towel he offered.

"Don't you go to school?" I asked.

"Yes, but it's close enough to walk. I keep my lunch in the fridge here and I come at noon every day to feed Spot and the red foots."

I looked around the room.

"In the corner behind the sink."

I bent down and saw two tortoises that looked like box turtles, only big and shaped like loaves of bread. They held their thick, scaly arms in close so that only their beak noses showed.

"Spike and Sammy. You could set your watch by when these guys show up to eat. One time I was late and they were at the door. Another five minutes and they would have come looking for me."

As Spot licked the dish for the last bits of fruit, I petted his back and around his shoulders. "You're lucky, Walter—I wish I had a place like this to be. The only pets I've ever had are back home in my grandpa's pond, down in the mud and ice and snow. I won't get to see them until summer."

"Don't you have *any* pets?"

"My mom has a cat."

Walter peeled a piece of dead skin off Spot's neck and rubbed it between his fingers. "Cats are nice. But they're not the same. When I touch a cat it's not the same as when I touch Badmouth."

"Who?"

"Badmouth, my retic? Reticulated python. Three years ago I found him outside the door in a pillowcase. He was as skinny and miserable-looking as a frayed old piece of rope, and he had the worst case of mouth rot I'd ever seen. Most of his lips are gone and his teeth hang out."

"Is he in one of the big boxes on top?"

"No, he's in my room. You've gotta come over and meet him. But that's why Spot can't go home with me. Iguanas are afraid of snakes, especially big ones."

Walter dropped the piece of skin from Spot's neck in the trash.

"Can I have that?"

Walter shrugged and retrieved the skin and gave it to me.

I held it in the palm of my hand. It was papery and see-through and a perfect impression of the place on Spot's neck where the scales were shaped like little cones.

"He has so many different scales."

"Yeah. The ones on his neck are pretty, but they're also like armor."

"For what, predators?"

"Maybe. In social interactions there's a lot of neck biting."

I looked at Spot, but I couldn't see him biting anything other than fruit. I tucked the skin inside my sweatshirt pocket.

Pops came back without the snake and wriggled his woolly eyebrows at me. He opened the door with the sign that said Do Not Feed the Alligators, went in, and shut the door behind him. I heard his footsteps going down stairs.

"Walter, where does that door go?"

"To the basement. The bathroom's down there and Pops's office and a lot of old snake cases and boxes of lightbulbs."

"Are there any alligators?"

"No. Well, we did have a caiman for a while, and some hot snakes."

"Hot?"

"Venomous. They're gone, too. It's just Pops down there, and a few loose geckos."

Henry started singing in the other room. "I guess I better go soon," I said.

"Will you come back tomorrow? I'll save his fruit again. You could help us with the animals, if you want."

"I'll come as soon as I get out of school."

The train going downtown wasn't so crowded. I got a seat in the corner, where I could be by myself.

It was nice, the way Walter invited me to see Badmouth, and I wanted to. But Badmouth wasn't mine and neither was Spot. It seemed kind of unfair that Walter got to have them both. I reached in my pocket and found the piece of skin and pressed it into my hand. The cone scales felt bumpy and a little bit sharp.

On Saturday it was freezing rain out and the sidewalks had patches of ice that were hard to see. Cathy called. "We can't go out walking in this," she said. "But you could come over here."

She told me how to get to her place, which was only a few blocks away. When I came around the corner I saw her standing outside her building, waving for me to hurry up.

I followed Cathy up five flights of stairs. I could hear Nitely whining on the other side of the door. As soon as it opened he was all over us, leaping and jumping, going back and forth between us, his tail spinning and wagging like he might explode. Cathy squatted and took his head in both hands so their noses touched. "What a good boy!"

He licked her face all over. They had been apart for maybe five minutes. Finally she stood up.

"Okay, boy," she said. He kept leaping up, trying to lick her some more. She patted his head and gently pushed him down. Keeping a hand on Nitely's head, Cathy took me into a wide-open room with high ceilings. "We have the whole top floor. We broke through into the other space for Dad's studio and the bedrooms. The kitchen's back here."

Nitely pranced around swinging his tail and looking up at Cathy. She reached into a box under the sink and pulled out a bone-shaped biscuit. He covered her hand with his mouth and crunched and chewed, and chunks of biscuit fell out the sides of his mouth suspended in strands of slobber. Then he went to his bowl and lapped up water, splashing all over and jingling the tags on his collar. When he lifted his head his muzzle was dripping. Cathy rubbed the top of his head and scratched around his ears. Then she took a handful of cookies out of the cookie jar and held one out to me.

I looked at it.

"You don't like Oreos?" she asked.

"No, I do. I'm just not hungry right now."

Cathy shrugged and popped the Oreo in her mouth. "Let's go back to my room. I have to share it with my sister, Ellen, but I think she's going out soon. Then we can watch a movie."

Cathy's sister sat cross-legged on her bed, watching TV. Her hair was blond like Cathy's, but wavy. She was wearing a black leotard like the ones dancers wear, and I could see how grown-up her body was.

She jerked her chin at me without taking her eyes off the television. "Who's this?"

"Grace. Where's Dad?"

"Where do you think?"

"My dad never comes out of his studio," Cathy told me. She held out the last Oreo. "Sure you don't want a cookie?"

I shook my head.

"You shouldn't either, Cath. You're getting fat."

Cathy stuck out her tongue at Ellen. "I'll get some more."

She left the room, Nitely at her heels. Ellen picked up a nail file and started working on her nails. I tried not to stare. On a table next to her bed I saw black candles stuck in bottles covered with dripped wax. I counted nine of them. The wicks were charred. A stuffed leather pouch lay on the table beside the candles.

Ellen paused to look at her nails. "You go to school with Cath?"

"Yeah."

"Same grade?"

"No, eighth." I looked at the shoes and clothes strewn around the room.

"Take off your jacket and relax."

I took off my jacket.

"Why don't you put it down somewhere, say, on the bed or the chair?"

I put my jacket on the chair.

Ellen kept filing and watching the television. "What are you guys up to?"

"I don't know."

"Sounds like fun."

Cathy came back with the package of cookies. She sat on the bed and kicked off her shoes. Nitely jumped up and sniffed the package.

"No, boy," Cathy said. "Sit." She patted the bed and he sat. "Grace, you too."

I looked at the pink bedspread with black dog hairs all over it. Cathy scooted over and pulled Nitely against her.

"Come on, there's plenty of room."

When I sat down Nitely got up and wagged his tail and

shoved his nose into my face and licked me. I jerked back and wiped my face.

"What's the matter?" Cathy said. "I get the feeling you don't like dogs."

"No, I like dogs."

I reached out to pet Nitely's head. He licked my hand and I wiped it on my jeans. Then he tried to lick my face again. I put my hand on his forehead and scratched between his ears. That stopped him. He sat down and panted, his tongue hanging out. I kept scratching his ears and steered his head a little to one side so his hot breath wouldn't be on my face.

"What are the candles for?" A drop of saliva was forming at the tip of the dog's tongue.

"Ellen's always burning black candles and pretending to put spells on people. She thinks she's a witch."

"Watch out, fatso, or I'll put one on you."

"Aren't you going out?"

Ellen smirked.

"Who with? I won't tell."

Ellen took her eyes off the TV for a second. "Like he'd care. Just friends."

"Yeah, right."

The drop of saliva fell and I flinched.

"What?"

"He's drooling."

"Dog drool won't kill you."

"I know, but it's sticky." Another drop was forming. I kept scratching his ears while I tried to scoot back a little. He raised his snout and touched my wrist with his nose, leaving a cool, wet spot.

"Nitely likes your friend, Cath," Ellen said.

"I thought you were going out. Nitely, move!" Cathy shoved against the dog's back, and finally he got down off the bed and curled up on the rug. "She's not going to give up the TV anytime soon," Cathy said to me. "We might as well draw."

She reached under the bed and pulled out a sketchbook and a box of pencils. She opened the sketchbook and showed me her drawings.

"That's Nitely at the beach last summer. And there he is with his chew toy."

She flipped through the pages to drawings of horses. Some stood with saddles on, but others were running or rearing up. They were perfectly drawn, with muscles and shading in the right places to make them look real.

"Move back a little," Cathy said.

She opened the sketchbook between us so we each had a blank page. She gave me a pencil, picked out one for herself, and started drawing. I sat holding the pencil. On my hand was a film of dog slobber. Cathy made two circles in the middle of the page and smaller ones below. Then she started connecting the circles with lines. Soon a horse was there, running across the paper. She drew the mane and a tail streaming out behind.

Cathy looked up. "Hey, Ellen. What do you think?"

Ellen aimed the remote and turned off the TV. She came and sat down on the bed with us. Seeing her grown-up body so close made me feel lucky that it hadn't happened to me.

"He's good, Cath. A little more shading here." Ellen pointed to the horse's neck. "Grace, why don't you draw?"

"All I can draw is frogs and snakes."

"Let's draw each other," Cathy said. "You first." She flipped the sketchbook to a blank page and pulled it onto her lap.

"I'm outta here," Ellen said.

"Look this way," Cathy said. "And hold still."

She looked at me, down at the sketchbook, up at me. Slowly her hand moved across the page and the pencil scrawled against the paper. She drew faster, biting her lip. Finally she stopped and leaned her head to the side.

"There." She turned the sketchbook around. Black lines made up a girl's face. The girl looked sad.

"I look like that?"

Cathy smiled. "Right now you do. Your turn to draw me."

"I can't draw people."

"You never tried." Cathy sat up straight and looked at me with her eyebrows raised, waiting. "Come on, practice."

I took the sketchbook. I picked up the pencil and looked at Cathy's face. Her eyes were green as a lizard. I drew them first. After that, nothing was like a lizard. Eyelashes, nose, hair, cheekbones, lips—all impossible.

"So how do I look?"

"I can't do this."

"Lemme see." She took the sketchbook. "That's not so bad. Just a little out of proportion, because you started with the eyes, I bet. Next time make an oval on the page. Eyes go in the middle."

"How did you learn to draw?"

"When we were little kids, before Mom left, Dad used to call us into his studio. He gave us our own sketchbooks and let us sit at his table. He used to paint these huge canvases that were so bright you could *feel* the greens and blues in them. He always had the classical station on the radio. Now, he doesn't want us to interrupt him."

"Where did your mother go?"

"She's in the south of France, living with some other artist."

"You don't miss her?"

"No."

I sat still. If my mother went away I could go back and be with my grandparents in Mooresville.

"Don't look so unhappy," Cathy said. "I'm perfectly fine."

When I saw the Nile monitor I couldn't take my eyes off him. I stood a little ways from the tank Walter was setting up. The lizard was speckled black and white, and he was big, with a belly thick as my arm. He had a long tail and a long neck, a head with a pointed snout, and large, restless eyes. His claws were curved and sharp. But it was the way he moved that I couldn't stop looking at.

"Where did he come from?"

"This kid brought him in here not half an hour ago. Said the lizard belonged to his brother, but he'd moved out. Three weeks went by before anyone realized the lizard was still in the guy's room."

I took a step closer. The lizard's eyes opened wide and I stopped. He flicked out his tongue. It was like a snake's, only longer and slower. The tiny scales all over his legs and body were like cloth that fit tight and showed his muscles and, in some places, his bones. A rough-looking patch of skin broke the black and white pattern all down his ribs. His neck arched as he turned to look at me. He flicked out his tongue again and again, lightly touching the brown paper he stood on. Muscles rippled underneath his skin as though he was ready to burst forward, yet he stayed calm. I never saw an animal who moved like that.

"He looks like the Komodo dragon at the museum."

"Same genus," Walter said. "*Varanus.* A cool group of lizards. All monitors can run, climb, burrow, and swim well."

"What are those funny black patches?"

"Sores from being kept in a dirty cage. That's why we've got him on the paper. Soon I need to get in there and treat them with antibiotic salve."

I took another step closer. The lizard puffed up his body, opened his mouth, and pushed out a sputtery hiss from down in his belly. He smacked the glass with his tail and I jumped. His eyelids flattened across the tops of his eyes, making them look furious.

"He's afraid," I said.

"Yeah. You don't want to put your hand in there. But if we're patient he may come around. Right now he needs a hide box."

Walter lifted one end of the screen and pushed a cardboard box with a hole in it down inside the tank. The monitor puffed himself up and hissed, but when he saw the opening in the box he flicked out his tongue, went inside, and turned himself around so that all of his tail went in. Walter set a heat lamp on top of the screen and switched it on.

"Tomorrow we'll try feeding him."

I wanted to feed him right away. I didn't know how Walter had the patience to wait. But I did know that if animals were upset, sometimes they threw up their food.

The next day the monitor was still inside his box. Walter had promised to wait for me before feeding him. I held up the screen while he pulled the forceps from his pocket and lowered a dead mouse into the tank. The monitor came out fast, flicking his tongue. He grabbed the mouse and shook the body hard, then dropped it and arched his neck, flicking his tongue in and out as though studying the mouse. I saw Walter cross his fingers. Finally the lizard took the mouse in his jaws and I heard a crunch. He tossed back his head, gulping, and the mouse went down his throat until only the tip of the tail showed, and that disappeared as the monitor bent his long neck and swallowed.

"He'll take another," Walter said.

He went into the back room and then returned with another mouse. Walter had given me my own forceps, and I pulled them from my back pocket. I looked at Walter. He held up the screen, and I took the mouse and lowered him into the tank. Fast as a snapping turtle the monitor struck. At the moment when he pulled the mouse from my forceps I got a rush of happiness to feel him take food.

By the following week the Nile monitor was resting partway out of his hide box, as though he wanted to see what was going on outside of his tank.

"He's feeling better for sure," Walter said. "Now those sores need attention."

Pops called out from the back room, "Need help, Walt?"

"No, we've got it."

Walter gave me a tube of antibiotic salve. As soon as he put his hand on top of the screen the monitor flicked out his tongue and raised his head. Walter lowered his hand onto the hide box and rested his knuckles there, with his fingers tucked in. The monitor climbed up and tongue-flicked Walter's hand again and again, but he didn't hiss. Slowly, Walter uncurled a finger and touched the lizard's throat. Then he eased his hand underneath the lizard's chest and held him for a minute.

"Okay, take the screen all the way off."

I did, and Walter reached in with his other hand, took hold of the monitor's hindquarters, and lifted him out. The lizard struggled and whipped his tail around and gave Walter a deep scratch across his wrist, but Walter pulled him in close and held on tight. I saw the muscles in Walter's arms.

"There now," he said, "you're okay."

The monitor calmed down and flicked out his tongue and blinked his eyes. Walter pulled the stepladder over with his foot and sat down. He cradled the lizard's body in his lap with his arm, supporting his chest in one hand while he stroked his back with the other.

"There, you see? You're safe." Walter held out his hand

toward me. "Grace, you want to open up that salve?"

I twisted off the cap and squeezed out some of the stuff onto Walter's fingers. He touched the salve to the sores, dabbing gently until all of them were covered. Walter didn't waste a second, returning the monitor to his tank the instant he was done. Right away the lizard went into his hide box.

"He understood you."

"Well, he doesn't understand my words, but he feels the tone of voice."

"What will happen to him? Are you going to sell him?"

Walter nodded. "We know a monitor fanatic. She's got a loft in Tribeca and a lot of money. I saw the place a few years ago, when Pops and I delivered a pair of Timors. It's all divided into custom-built rooms that are climate-controlled. They're perfect habitats, with plants and small trees, even. Some are hot and dry, for Perenties and Savannahs. Some are humid, for Dumeril's and black-throats. A couple of the rooms actually have pools for Salvators and Niles. That's where he's going." Then he took the salve and smeared some on the scratch the monitor had given him.

"Lucky lizard."

"Yeah, I guess he is." Walter picked up the screen and settled it noiselessly on top of the tank.

Now and then a customer asked about the monitor, but Walter said he wasn't for sale. And when the lizard went to his new home I was happy for him. But I missed his fierce eyes and the way he watched us working around the shop.

"I miss him too," Walter said. "But you know, it's hard, keeping carnivores and herbivores in the same room."

"What?"

Walter smiled. "Monitors and iguanas shouldn't be kept together. You want to feed the Pyxie?"

"Sure," I said.

I loved to feed *Pyxiecephalus*, the African bullfrog. He was three times the size of my Mooresville bullfrog, with a yellow throat and bumpy olive skin, and he would eat until he exploded, I was sure. Walter gave me a dead mouse. I took out my forceps and held the mouse in front of the frog. His throat drummed quicker, his eyes grew, and all of a sudden he snatched the mouse in his jaws and stuffed the back legs in with his thumbs. He blinked hard and gulped the mouse down. Whenever I watched the animals eat I was glad the food animals were dead already.

"How do you kill the rodents?"

"Come in the back," Walter said, as though he'd been waiting for me to ask.

He held a rat gently and wrapped his thumb and fingers around the neck while he took the base of the tail in his other hand. In one quick motion he tightened his hold on the rat's neck and yanked on the head. The rat's body lay across Walter's hand, head hanging loose, whiskers still, dark pink eyes open.

"Snaps his neck instantly," he said. The look on his face was a mix of kindness and resolve.

He took out his forceps and lowered the rat by the scruff of his neck in front of Sue, the Burmese python. She raised her head, tongue flicking in and out fast, her coils moving like gears starting to spin, pushing her neck into an *S* behind her head. Sue hit the rat hard and pulled him into a tight coil. The rat's eyes bulged and his nose turned gray-blue.

After a few minutes Sue unhooked her teeth from the rat. She flicked her tongue over his body until she found his nose. Then she opened her mouth wide and closed it around the rat's head. Her jaws moved like they were walking over the body. When the rat was halfway down she raised her head. Her chin and neck were so stretched out that the scales were spread apart and pink skin showed between them. I could see her throat muscles ripple, pulling the rat down to her stomach. His tail disappeared like a piece of spaghetti being sucked in.

Sometimes I held Sue. At two and a half years old, she was already as long as I am tall and as thick as my calf. Her scales were as big and smooth as the nail on my little finger, and the ones on her head were like tiles of various shapes that fit together in a pattern. When she wrapped her muscular body around me, it felt like being hugged all over. After a while she would always start pulling toward the floor, wanting to go somewhere.

"If you turned her loose," Walter told me, "she'd find that hole behind the pipes and go down into the guts of the building to hunt rats."

Some days I held Pete the pine snake and worked around the shop with him tangled in my hair. But eventually he wanted to go exploring, like Sue, only he would reach out, not down, and try to climb onto the top of another animal's tank. When the small lizards saw him doing that, they scattered and bumped into their glass walls.

Walter said the old boa constrictor, Mr. Boa, was old enough to be my father, even though he was small for a snake his age. He was the one I could hold while I did things, like spray-mist the anoles and tree frogs and change water bowls. He didn't try to go anywhere, he just kept himself coiled in close, wrapped around my shoulders with his head tucked under my chin and his tail curled in the belt loop on my jeans. The scales on his head were like tiny beads, and the brown and black stripy blotches on his face made him look like he was wearing a mask.

The best thing of all, though, was being with Spot. Something inside me melted every time I saw him. I loved his lizard face, and I wanted to hold him and feel his scaly lips against mine. I brought him blueberries and ripe plums from the market and then sat on the counter next to the sink and held him in my lap while I fed him the fruit and wiped juice from his lips with my thumb and finger. I petted under his chin and around his neck, where the tiny scales felt like silk. He flicked my hands and my jeans with his tongue as though he was finding out about me. And when I kissed him he always flicked out his salty tongue at the right moment.

Walter had a key to a cabinet with glass doors where tarantulas and scorpions lived inside big round jars. He showed me how the black scorpion glowed green under a black light, and how to hold the Mexican red legs tarantula. If I let her fall, her belly would break open like an egg.

"What's inside the jar on top, the one that's all white?"

"A spider from Brazil," he said. "We finally got her to eat, but I don't know if she can adapt. The white stuff is silk she's closed herself in with."

"None of the other spiders do that."

"No, they seem fine. Some have made egg sacs, even. The baby red legs are the cutest—just little black and orange fuzz balls at first."

The white jar bothered me. All those silk threads spun to cover every bit of glass so that nobody could see in, or maybe so the spider didn't have to see out. I wondered how to reach her and tell her not to be so afraid. I woke up in the night with the dream of being on a plane and parachuting down into the rain forest to open the jar and let the spider out. I wanted to do that so much it made my chest ache and my eyes sting.

Since it was getting warmer, Cathy wanted to go to the park on Saturdays and play handball. She tied Nitely outside the fence, where he sat and waited the whole time we played. Every so often Cathy called out, "Good boy!" and Nitely would stand up and wag his tail and shake himself all over.

Cathy always brought the ball, which was the size of an apple and like a tough sponge. It made a satisfying *thop* when we smacked it into the side of the building. After warming up a while we'd start a game. When one of us hit the ball too hard it went over our heads and bounced around the park until it was gritty with dirt. The worst was when it rolled into the puddle of brown water in the corner and I had to get it out with the toe of my sneaker. My hands got sooty and started itching and I tried not to think about the dog droppings and other icky stuff that was around.

I started to like playing handball, though. After we had played a while, my heart beat fast and my face felt warm.

Cathy would look at me and say, "This is a great way to work out your anger."

I didn't think I was angry, but I did feel a lot better after playing handball.

One day we were in the middle of a game when this girl showed up. She was short but tough-looking, with black eyes. I felt as though a storm cloud had moved in. She stood on the sideline and bounced a ball, watching us play. I missed my shot.

"I play winner," she said.

Cathy caught the ball and stopped the game. "Yeah, okay. We're almost through. Iris, this is Grace."

Iris stared at me. I could tell she was looking at my jacket. I frowned back at her.

"I hate snakes," she said.

Cathy threw the ball at me. "Let's finish the game."

I tossed the ball back to Cathy and she served. I smacked it back hard.

"Take it easy, Grace."

"I'm working out my anger."

It went like that until I lost. I walked off the court and stood outside the fence with Nitely while Cathy and Iris played.

When they were done and Cathy and I were walking home, I said, "I don't like that girl."

"Iris is okay."

"She's not very nice."

"You weren't very nice to her, either."

"She said she hates snakes. She gave me a mean look."

"You should've seen the look you gave her."

"Well, I don't like how she makes me feel—like I don't belong there."

"I think it's really up to you, whether you feel like you belong or not."

Cathy was right and it made me mad, because I didn't know how to fix the way I felt.

Before leaving Fang & Claw on Friday, I asked Walter to come play handball in the park with us. "I'm no good at sports," he said.

"That doesn't matter."

"Usually I do homework on Saturdays."

"Me too, except when Cathy drags me out to the park. But it's fun, really."

"I don't know. Anyway, see you Monday?"

"Yeah, but it's the park downtown on Thompson Street, okay?"

"Okay. Maybe."

—

I looked at the fence again to see if Walter was there. Cathy said, "You're keeping a close watch on Nitely today."

"Yeah," I said, smacking the ball. We'd been playing for over an hour, I figured.

"Your friend is here."

I turned around, but it was Iris. She ruffed Nitely's fur and scratched his ears before coming in through the gate.

"Hey, guys," she said.

Cathy served and I missed. I had to run over by the fence and get the ball.

"Nineteen, seventeen," Cathy said.

"You letting her win again?" Iris said to me. "What's the matter, you scared to play me?"

"I'm not scared."

I threw the ball to Cathy and she served. I returned the shot and we played and I scored a point. But I hit the next shot too hard and it went way over my head.

"I'll get it," Iris said. "Use mine." She threw a ball at me and I caught it. The ball was new and still pink.

"Thanks," I said.

Cathy slapped me on the arm. "See?"

I served Iris's ball. We got a volley going, but finally Cathy scored and won the game.

Iris shook her head. "How will I ever get to play you?"

I shrugged; I couldn't think of what to say. I went over by the fence and bent to tighten my shoelaces. Nitely's leash jingled the way it did when someone was petting him, and I turned to see who was there.

"Nice dog," Walter said.

"Walter, you made it!"

"I finished my homework. Thought I'd come say hi."

He had on his Bronx Zoo Reptile House T-shirt and khaki shorts that went down to his knees. It was funny to see him outside of Fang & Claw.

Cathy came over. "That's Nitely. I'm Cathy."

"This is my friend Walter, from Fang & Claw."

Iris wrinkled her nose. "Fang & Claw?"

"Walter's pet shop. He has lots of snakes."

Iris bounced her ball and looked at Walter. "You play handball?"

He put his hands in his pockets. "Maybe I better watch."

"No way," Cathy said. She took the ball from Iris and bounced it. "You and Grace against us."

We started a game. I bent my knees and got ready, and I moved fast when it was my turn.

"Oh, look out," Iris said. "Grace is serious."

Walter kept missing the ball. I watched him run after it. His legs were so white.

Iris rolled her eyes and put a fist on her waist. "God, you're slow."

"Sorry." Walter's face was red and his shoulders sagged.

I glared at Iris and missed a shot. The ball rolled over by the fence, and when I went to get it I saw the biggest cockroach ever. He was on his back, a shiny chestnut color, with his wings folded under him. His legs had spines on them and his eyes were round and black. One of his long antennae moved.

"He's alive!" I could see how he was breathing, his body pulsing in and out. He moved his legs, trying to turn himself over, but he couldn't.

Walter came up beside me. "He's been poisoned. Look away and I'll kill him."

I turned my head. Walter's sneaker scraped the cement quick.

"Oh, gross," Iris said.

Cathy laughed. "You two are weird."

"When were you going to tell me about Fang & Claw?" Cathy asked. She sat on the mattress, stuffing a pillow into a pillowcase. We were making up a bed in my loft so she could sleep over. Nitely lay curled on a blanket at the foot of the ladder.

"I did tell you, remember? I told you about Spot. The lizard I painted on my jacket?"

"Yeah, but what about Walter? You like him, don't you."

"I do?"

Cathy threw the pillow at me. "He definitely likes you."

"How do you know?"

"Because he came out to see you. A guy like that doesn't just go to the park on a Saturday."

"Yeah, well, I did invite him. What do you mean, 'a guy like that'?"

"Come on, Grace. He's not much to look at, and that's putting it nicely."

"So?" I said.

"Aha! You *do* like him!"

I threw the pillow back at Cathy and she laughed at me. My mother tapped on the door and poked her head in. "Girls? I'm leaving now. Don't answer the phone and don't open the door for anyone."

I could tell she was going someplace nice, because she had put on earrings and shoes with high heels. We listened to the door shutting, the lock clicking, and her footsteps going down the stairs.

Cathy sat up straight. "Let's put a hex on Ellen."

"What?"

"You know, a spell. To make something happen to her." Cathy's eyes got big.

"I don't think I want to do that."

"We're not going to kill her, just give her a rash or something."

"Why?"

"Because she's always going around threatening to put a hex on me. And Friday night she took my only dress without asking and she wore it on one of her dates and ruined it. Then she acted like it was nothing. 'You're getting too fat for it anyway,' she said."

"Well, okay," I said. "As long as we don't use any toad parts."

"No, silly, we don't use toad parts, or bat tongues or spider legs. All we need is one of Ellen's black candles." Cathy started down the ladder, and Nitely got all excited and pranced around.

"What if my mother comes back and we're not here? I don't want to get in trouble."

"The way she was dressed, she'll be out late. Sit, Nitely." Cathy hooked the leash on his collar. "Let's go."

It had rained, and the traffic lights made blurry red and green reflections on the wet streets and on the windows of stores shut down for the night.

"This way," Cathy whispered, pulling me down a side street. We walked quickly, in silence, except for the jingling of Nitely's leash. He kept having to stop and sniff around signposts and lift his leg. "Nitely!" Cathy hissed. "Hurry up." Then she started humming the theme song from *Mission: Impossible*. I looked over at her and she cracked up laughing.

All the lights were out at Cathy's. TV voices came from her dad's studio, where blue-white light made a thin line in the shape of a door in the wall. We walked back to Cathy's room and she turned on the light. Clothes and a wet towel were heaped on Ellen's bed. Cathy dropped to her knees and pulled a flat box from under the bed. Inside were the black candles. She took one and gave it to me.

"Won't she know we took it?"

"Who cares? Let's go." She closed the box, shoved it back under the bed, and stood. "Wait! We can't forget the personal object."

"The what?"

"We need something of hers to burn for the spell to work. Fingernails are best, but we don't have those." Cathy looked around the room, then down at the floor. She picked up a black sock. "This will do."

"You're going to burn that?"

"Oh, yes." She cackled like a witch and stuffed the sock in the pocket of her jeans.

"But she'll know."

"She'll know what, that we took a sock and burned it to hex her? I doubt it."

We ran all the way back, up the stairs two at a time, in the door, and up the ladder to my loft. Catching her breath, Cathy twisted the base of the candle into a soda bottle and set it on a book. She took the sock out of her pocket and placed it next to the candle.

"Get something to hold it with."

I went back down to the kitchen and looked at the utensils. The wooden spoon would burn and a regular one was too short. Then I saw the serving fork—a long one with two tines and a black handle.

Cathy sat cross-legged and motioned for me to do the same. She struck a match and lit the candle between us. She closed her eyes and started going, "Mmm."

"What are you doing?"

She opened one eye and said, "Shhh!" and shut it again. "Come on. You too."

We both went, "Mmm," but I kept one eye open. I started feeling dumb, and I wished she would hurry up and get to the burning part so we could be done with it. I kept worrying that my mother would come home any minute.

"Okay," Cathy said, finally. "Burn it."

I picked up the sock on the end of the fork and held it over the flame. It caught fire. The fire burned bright and Cathy's smile was all lit up and spooky. But as the flame died, the smoke turned black and smelled bad, like burning plastic.

The sock didn't burn up into nothing; it started melting and sizzling and dripping on the book cover.

Cathy blew out the flames. "Uh-oh. It was synthetic."

A smoldering black lump stuck to the end of the fork and the drops of stuff that had fallen cooled into hard globs. We looked at each other in the light from the street lamp. A wisp of smoke rose from the charred wick.

"What did we do to her?" I asked.

"Any day now, she'll start itching uncontrollably." Cathy smiled.

I narrowed my eyes at her. "Did you really know what you were doing?"

"Nah. I watched Ellen put a hex on her math teacher once, and it was sort of like that. I had you going, though, huh?"

"You mean you did all this to fool me?"

"I was just messing around. Loosen up! Admit it—we had fun. Anyway, we need to practice so we can put a love spell on Walter."

"No, you can't!"

One day I was in the back room with Spot when Walter and Pops came in. They stood side by side, smiling at me.

Walter put his hands in the pockets of his jeans. "We want you to have Spot," he said.

I looked at Walter, then at Pops. I stayed calm. "For real?"

"Yep," Pops said. "Okay. Back to work." He smiled again at me and went up front.

"But Walter, won't you miss him?"

"Sure. I have Badmouth, though." He reached over and held the long toes of Spot's foot. "He can't spend his life back here."

"When can I take him?"

"Today. Pops called your mom. She's coming to help get his cage and things into a taxi."

I hugged Spot and leaned my cheek against his shoulder. Walter took the water bowl out of the cage and emptied it in the sink.

"Will you come here anymore?"

"Of course. I'll come here first, right after school. Or maybe I'll go feed Spot and then come. I'll definitely be here."

That night we pushed Spot's cage up the ladder. I hurried around getting the cage ready while my mother sat on the bed holding Spot in her lap and studying him through her glasses.

"I can't get over the colors. There are so many shades of each—it's too many to count."

I fiddled with the basking branch, propping it in one corner and then another until it had the right angle. I twisted the Vitalite and heat bulbs into their fixtures and filled his water bowl, and the cage was ready. My mother was petting Spot.

"I always thought of lizards as little creatures that scurried away," she said.

"Now you can see why I wanted him, huh?"

"Sure I can. But you'll have your hands full."

I took Spot from my mother and put him in the cage. He

climbed up his branch and turned his head slowly, looking around. I shut the cage door and hated it.

Right after dinner I went back up to Spot. He looked okay. But I couldn't bear to leave him in there, so I opened the door and lifted him out and hugged him.

I pulled back the blanket and put Spot down on my bed. His claws made creases in the sheet that fanned out like huge hands. I put on my nightgown and got under the covers with him. He flicked the pillow and my arm with his tongue. I petted his back and touched each spine in his crest all the way down his tail. He settled himself, letting his chin rest, tucking his arms back along his sides. I touched his scaly palms and the claws curving up at the end of each finger. He shut his eyes. I pulled the blanket up over us and turned off the light. I held Spot close and kissed him. I wanted so much for him to know that I loved him.

I must have moved away in the night, because I felt his cool body pressed against my back, pulling heat from me. I rolled over and held him and soon we were both warm again.

In the gray morning light I stared at the big lizard asleep beside me, unable to believe that he was mine, for always. I looked at his ears, like ovals of parchment, and the skin of his eyelids with scales so tiny it was like fine cloth. Two single scales formed a ring around each nostril. I touched the soft folds of his dewlap and felt the thin bone inside that he pushed it out with when he wanted to make himself bigger. He opened his eyes and sneezed and started licking his lips to clean his teeth, making a soft clicking sound. I kissed him on the nose and went down the ladder to fix breakfast. I sliced a banana and put half on my cereal and half on his collard-and-dandelion salad, and we ate breakfast in bed.

But on weekdays Spot had to eat breakfast in his cage. I worried about how little there would be for him to do all day when he was by himself. If I took him to school with me he could sit in my lap while I studied. He would ride on my shoulder with his spiky dragon crest sticking up and his long tail hanging down. He would hate the subway, though.

I told my mother Spot needed green leaves around him, so he could feel as though he was in the rain forest. She gave me her big hibiscus plant. He loved it so much that he sat on it and broke the branches and ate the leaves. Then we bought a pothos plant and put it outside the cage, so the vines made a leafy curtain.

Whenever I was home Spot was out of the cage. And when he wasn't sitting on my shoulder, he climbed all over my dresser and the clothes in my closet. His claws made holes in the fabric, but I didn't care. It was hard to do homework when he was climbing around and knocking things over, though. He needed a place to be up high, a place of his own, where he could sit while I worked. I found some heavy twine and tied both ends of a flannel sheet to make a hammock. Then I stood on my desk in the corner and hammered a nail in each wall and strung the hammock between them. Inside it I put a heating pad turned on low. As soon as I set Spot up there, he quit trying to climb any higher. He tilted his head to look down at me sitting at my desk. When he sneezed, it felt like a cool mist falling. It left specks of dried salt on the pages of my books.

—

After the long days of spring came, I had time with Spot after school and then I could go over to Fang & Claw for a couple of hours. Walking in the city I caught the earth smell seeping up through cracks in the cement and wherever a tree grew. Even with exhaust in the air I smelled the warm green of summer coming. It made my stomach tremble with excitement about going home to Mooresville for vacation. I could just about feel grass and mud on my bare feet and hear warm, humid nights ringing with frog and bug song. My head was so filled up with Mooresville that there wasn't any room for thoughts about coming back to the city when summer was over.

Saturday morning Spot was basking in a patch of sunlight on my bed when Cathy showed up. He sneezed and Nitely growled.

"What's that?"

"Spot."

"Spot?" Cathy went up the ladder. "Oh God, there's a lizard in your bed!"

"I told you about him."

"Yeah, but I thought you meant a little gecko or something. This thing's huge. Will it attack?"

"I don't think so."

"You don't *think* so?"

"I don't think he'll like the smell of Nitely on you, but no, he won't attack. Go up, you're blocking the way."

Cathy sat down at the foot of the bed. Spot pushed out his dewlap.

"It's looking at me."

"Of course he is." I put my hand on Spot's back.

"What's that thing under its chin—that flap it keeps pushing out?"

"His dewlap. He does that to make himself look bigger."

"What, to scare me?"

"Or impress you." I pulled Spot into my lap and he relaxed his dewlap. "Why don't you pet him?"

Cathy put out her hand and then jerked it back when Spot tongue-flicked her finger.

"He's just smelling you."

"You sure?"

"I'm sure."

Slowly Cathy reached out, away from Spot's head, and touched his back. "It feels rough."

"Try here, around his neck."

"That's okay." She drew up her legs and hugged her knees. Nitely whined and thumped his tail against the ladder.

Spot climbed up to my shoulder and I leaned my cheek against him.

"He's actually pretty cool," Cathy said. "But what do you do with him? Don't you want a pet you can snuggle up with? Something warm and furry?"

"I snuggle with Spot."

I looked at Cathy over the spines of his crest. She shook her head. "You're weird."

"What's so weird about that?"

"Don't get upset, I like weird. But with that cage up here,

there's no room for me. I guess you'll just have to sleep over at my house."

"I don't think Ellen likes me."

"Oh, she does too. Anyway, why do you care?"

"It's sort of uncomfortable when she's there."

"Ellen's been gone almost every weekend and you haven't stayed over once. Come next Friday—it's the last day of school and we can celebrate before you go."

"Saturday. Friday's Fang & Claw."

On my last day at Fang & Claw I filled the spray bottle with water and gave the tree frogs their misting. It had been one of my favorite things to do all through the winter. I would stand still, looking in at the moss and the leaves, shiny green and dripping, and smell the damp orchid bark and imagine I was in there with the frogs in the forest after a rainstorm.

Walter said, "You're excited about going back for vacation, huh?"

"Yeah, I can't wait to show Spot grass and trees and the pool. He'll eat turnip greens and collards out of the garden and wild dandelion flowers and all the blueberries he wants, right off the bush."

"It sounds great. Just be careful you don't lose him. Sunlight can make lizards go wild."

When it was time to go I caught myself feeling sad.

"Say hi to your bullfrog," Walter said.

"I will. Did you ever go to the country?"

"I've been to California and down through Mexico."

"You would like Mooresville."

"I know I would."

I left Fang & Claw and before turning the corner I looked back and saw Walter standing at the gate, waving goodbye.

Saturday night Cathy buzzed me in. I hated leaving Spot home alone, but I wouldn't get to see Cathy all summer. I started climbing the stairs. Above me I heard the lock click, the door swing open, and Cathy yell, "Go see!"

The whole stairway shook with Nitely's barking and leash jangling and toenails clattering. We reached the fourth floor landing at the same time and I gripped the handrail as he leapt against me, licking and pawing and wagging his tail.

"Down, boy," Cathy said. She stood at the top of the stairs in a big T-shirt and socks. "Where's your stuff?"

"Stuff?"

"Toothbrush, pajamas?"

"I forgot."

"I've got sweats you can wear. Come on!"

With Nitely at her heels, she went running and gliding across the polished wood floor and skated to a stop with her hand on the refrigerator door handle.

"Ellen's still here. But look what I made."

Cathy yanked open the door and pulled out a plate stacked with brownies.

"The cold makes them chewy."

Nitely leapt for the brownies. Cathy held the plate high. "Down, boy. I hope you like nuts in them. Some people don't."

"I like nuts."

"Grab a soda. Get me one too. They're in the door."

I took the sodas, shut the fridge, and followed Cathy back to her room. Ellen was stretched out on her bed in cutoffs and a T-shirt, holding the TV remote.

Cathy set the plate of brownies on the dresser, then hopped up on her bed and crossed her legs. I hung my jacket on the bedpost. Cathy brushed some dog hair off the blanket.

"Sit, you guys."

Nitely jumped up and I sat down beside him.

"Lie down, boy. Nitely will keep our feet warm tonight."

I managed to keep Nitely away from my brownie, but he licked the top of my soda can. I put it down on the floor. Cathy swatted Nitely on the butt.

"Nitely, lie down. Hey, Ellen, I thought you were going out."

Ellen yawned. She struck a match, lit one of her black candles, and blew out the match.

Cathy sighed. "Well, can we at least watch a movie?"

Ellen aimed the remote at the TV and changed the channel. Nitely panted and drooled. His tail thumped the bed every time we made eye contact. I felt terrible, because he was a nice dog. His brown eyes searched mine, wanting us to be friends. I liked him, I really did, I just didn't like touching him and I hated it when he touched me.

"Come *on*, Ellen," Cathy said. "Let's watch a movie."

"Give me a brownie."

"Get your own."

"Wanna watch a movie?"

"Okay, okay."

Ellen put out her hand. Cathy got up and took a brownie to her sister.

Ellen took a bite and chewed it slowly. "We can watch *Titanic,* which is half over, or *Alien,* which is just starting."

"I hate watching half-over movies," Cathy said.

Ellen changed the channel and put down the remote. "Shut the lights."

Cathy went to the closet, pulled a T-shirt and sweatpants off the shelf, and dropped them in my lap. She turned off the light, then sat down beside me and tugged on my shoelace. My sneaker came loose and I kicked it off.

It didn't take long for Cathy to fall asleep. She slept right through the part where the baby alien burst out of the man's chest and everyone was screaming. Ellen turned down the volume after that.

I was having a hard time getting comfortable, with all the covers twisted around and the stuffy dog smell and Nitely's weight making my feet sweat, and I thought it would wake Cathy if I rolled around too much. I couldn't stop worrying about Spot, either, alone in his cage. Finally I couldn't stand it any longer. I pulled my feet out from under Nitely and crept out of bed and started putting on my sneakers.

"What's the matter?" Cathy said, suddenly coming awake.

"I need to go home."

"You're kidding. It's the middle of the night."

Ellen giggled.

"Shut up," Cathy said.

I tied my shoes. Ellen kept giggling.

"Would you stop?"

Ellen pulled the covers over her face.

"Tell me why, Grace."

"I'm worried about Spot."

"Oh, please, you can't leave him for one night?"

"He gets lonely."

"So you'd rather be with a lizard."

Ellen dropped the covers. "Hey, wait—this is better than *Alien*. You sleep with a lizard? What's that like?"

Cathy threw her pillow at Ellen. "Will you lay off!" Then she blew out a breath. "All right, all right. I'll walk you." She got up, put on a sweatshirt, and stepped into her clogs. "Nitely, you stay."

I hurried down the stairs ahead of Cathy and pushed open the door. We walked in silence except for Cathy's clogs, clopping on the sidewalk. She took off her sweatshirt and tied it around her waist.

"Can you tell me why you can sleep with a giant lizard but dog drool freaks you out?"

"I was born that way," I said, finally. Then I thought, I bet Walter would say that about himself.

"What are you smiling about?"

"Nothing."

"Yeah, right."

"I'm just looking forward to going home. I can't wait to see Spot in the garden."

Cathy put her arm through mine.

"When you come back we'll have the best time. Ellen's going away to college and I'll have the room to myself. And things will be so much better next fall when we're both in the upper school."

I didn't say anything. In the back of my mind I was hoping that something would happen—I didn't know what, but something—so I wouldn't have to come back. We stopped at my door.

"Bet you'll miss me," Cathy said.

"Yeah, I will. You could come to Mooresville."

"Nah. I've got Nitely. Besides, summer is great in the city."

"How can you say it's great when it's dirty and hard and people are everywhere? I don't get it! I don't want to come back—I can't deal with being here."

"Yes, you can!" Cathy said, throwing her arms around me. "Because I am helping you." Cathy let go of me after a minute. "Feel better?"

"Yeah. Thanks for walking me. Sorry I couldn't stay, but …"

"You're totally weird."

My mother woke up when I came in, and I told her that I was sneezing at Cathy's because of all the dog hair. I went to my room and lifted Spot from his cage and took him to bed. Under the covers, I pulled him onto me and he pressed his rough, scaly belly to mine. I could feel his body taking heat from me. His chin settled on my chest and he tucked back his arms.

I played with his claws. Soon my breath moved in and out, steady with his. I ran my finger down his crest of spines that felt like quills on a young bird. Down on his tail the scale ridge was so sharp it could tear skin if I touched it the wrong way. It made me squirm, thinking about how Ellen wanted to make something weird out of me sleeping with Spot. I rolled onto my side and held him close. Breathing his lizard smell made me lightheaded. I felt safe. I reached under my pillow and touched the plane ticket.

Mooresville

When I was little, I took Grandpa ice water whenever I saw him out riding his tractor in the hot sun. It took him the whole afternoon to cut the grass, driving his tractor around the house in circles that grew bigger until they met the woods. Sweat rolled down his face and into the folds of his bare, suntanned belly, and his silvery hair lay across the top of his head in thin, wet strips. I could feel how thirsty he must be. So I would run and fill one of Grandma's canning jars with ice water and carry it out across the field to meet the tractor. I would get so excited, waiting for the moment when he saw me and his face lit up. He would start pushing on pedals and levers and the tractor would stop. I would hold up the jar of water and he'd take a long drink and go, "Aaahh!" and put the empty jar down in the toolbox under the seat.

Then he would say, "Put your foot on that step," and he'd reach down and take my arm and pull me into his lap. He'd take his foot off the pedal and pull up on the lever, and the tractor would start up and jerk forward. He'd have both his arms around me, his hands on the steering wheel. He'd pull another lever and the bush hog would drop back down and start whirring, and the smells of cut grass and tractor engine and Grandpa's sweat would fill me up. And he'd sing, "Here comes Peter Cottontail, hopping down the bunny trail!"

Grandpa sang the Easter song no matter what time of year it was. He knew Easter was my favorite—better than Christmas, even. Easter was when the robins returned and the frogs woke up and the turtles came out. But it wasn't quite summer and the dogwood buds weren't open yet, just fat, and everything was getting started and it was all still ahead.

—

I had a window seat on the airplane. From up here Manhattan looked like a spiky cluster of concrete towers and blocks speckled with glistening bits that were the windows. I loved watching everything get smaller and smaller, fading out of sight. Below, the grid of streets and houses was giving way to trees and hills. I pressed my face against the window and peered into the distance ahead to see the thin line of green.

Summer had already started and all the animals would be feeding babies in nests or burying eggs by the pond. I wondered if it would be really hot.

I remembered when we had hot spells, with a white hazy sky forever and each day holding a charge, like a thunderstorm about to happen. Nobody could stand to have any clothes on. Grandma would weed the flowerbeds in her bathing suit, humming, sweat running down her cheeks. Grandpa would go down to work in the garden wearing only his old blue trousers that were so worn out they looked like lace in some places. In nothing but my shorts, I would jump in the pool and then go running down the path through the woods, skipping over tree roots and stones until I reached the pond. Even in that heat we ate our meals on the porch, because no one wanted to be apart from the woods and the bird and frog songs.

When the plane landed and came to a stop at the gate, I felt like I had tadpoles wriggling inside. I saw Grandma first, standing there with her purse strap over one shoulder and her arms folded, watching people getting off the plane. Then we saw each other and hugged, and for a second I thought she had gotten shorter.

"Your plane was right on time." She nodded at the pet carrier. "Got your friend in there?"

"Uh-huh."

"Your grandfather is waiting in the car." Grandma put her arm through mine and we headed for the baggage claim.

Grandpa got out of the car and gave me a hug. "You grew up."

Grandma drove while Grandpa looked out the window. He whistled his old college football cheer and patted his knee to keep time. I rode in the back seat, holding Spot's carrier on my lap, watching barns and farmhouses and fields of corn and soybeans go by. Some fields had clusters of new houses, like patches of big weeds cropping up. I looked out the other window at traffic going back toward the airport, and I remembered last fall when my mother got really homesick. We took the first flight we could get and Grandma and Grandpa picked us up at the airport. My mother kept crying and Grandma hugged her and patted her and I was so happy—I was sure that we would move back home. But two days later we were driving down that other side of the highway and they put us on a plane back to the city. I didn't talk the whole time. My mother didn't care; she read her books and got ready for the next school day as if nothing had happened.

Finally we exited the highway and drove through town. I thought Grandma had taken a wrong turn, because a gas station stood where the general store was supposed to be.

"See the new Texaco?" she said. "They tore down the general store, since everyone goes to the mall now."

Passing by the new gas station I counted twelve pumps.

We followed Route 42 out of town and I leaned forward to watch for the sign, a rough old board nailed to the phone pole with KELLER HILL ROAD painted in white letters. The road took us through a cornfield and into the woods. I rolled down the window and breathed in the moist, green smells of summer in the country. It made my throat tight.

Up the road the woods gave way to more cornfields as we drove by the Rummel and Platt farms and then on into more woods. Abruptly the woods ended, and I sat straight up in my seat. Grandma slowed the car. A new house stood at the edge of a wide field of bare ground.

"What happened?" I asked. "Where are the Prescotts?"

Grandma looked at me in the rearview mirror. "'Soon as Tootie died, the kids sold the property and moved away."

A car came up behind, honked, and went around us.

I sat still and watched a bulldozer push a tree stump, its roots sticking up in the air with clods of earth falling away. Nearby sat another house in two halves, all wrapped up in plastic.

People were already living in the finished house. A bicycle lay on its side in patchy new grass and a square of blue light glowed behind the curtains.

Grandma drove the car on up the road toward Keller Hill. I scooted over to look out at the place where the creek disappeared to go under the road. On the other side, it came pouring from the end of a culvert pipe and showered down into a pool surrounded by rocks. One of them was flat and perfect for sitting. I liked to go down there and sit on that rock with the turtles and snakes and frogs. As we passed by I saw that a guardrail had been put in.

"You have to be careful, Grace, when you take a walk to the creek," Grandma said. "Seems like every day more and more cars come flying down this hill ninety miles an hour."

At the top of the hill Grandma turned in to the driveway. I forgot about traffic on Keller Hill Road the moment I saw the house. Cradled by the gentle-sloping hill and tucked in by dogwood trees and ivy beds, the house looked as though it had been waiting for me. I saw the giant wisteria, its thick vines twisted and wrapped around the posts of my bedroom balcony, making it like a treehouse. As we came closer I saw the ever-green bushes around the living room windows, where praying mantis egg cases would have already hatched, releasing tiny replicas of their parents. And when we pulled up to the garage I saw the flowerbeds loaded with fat white peonies and purple and yellow irises. Toads burrowed in the flowerbed mulch to keep their bodies moist during the day, but tonight I would see them hopping around the patio, hunting bugs.

"What happened to the lilac bushes?"

"They blighted," Grandma said. "We had to have Bob Ellis come take them out."

Grandpa held the door while I brought my suitcase and pet carrier into the air-conditioned house. It smelled faintly of chlorine from the pool and of tomato sauce cooking, which was funny, since tomatoes weren't ripe until July. Right away I needed to get out of my city clothes and shoes. I hurried up the stairs to my room with my things and pulled the door shut behind me. The room was golden with light from the setting sun, and shadows from wisteria leaves made patterns on the walls. I set the carrier on my bed and lifted the lid. With Spot in my arms, I went to the balcony doors and opened them to let in the warm, humid air. In the crook of the wisteria branches a robin's nest was stuffed so full of sleeping baby birds I thought it might burst. The heap of pinfeathers and bill tips moved up and down with the babies' breathing. Frogs began to sing down at the pond.

Spot and I touched noses. "We're home," I whispered. We stood still and listened to the frogs a while before going back inside.

I fished around in my suitcase and pulled out the heat mat and plugged it in. Spot settled himself on the mat and flicked it with his tongue. He blinked and looked at the leaf shadows on the wall.

After I kicked off my sneakers I saw how filthy and out of place they were on the white carpet. I picked them up by the laces and dropped them in the closet. I took off my shirt and jeans, put on shorts and a T-shirt, and went downstairs.

The table in the dining room was set, with candles and a tablecloth and wine glasses.

"Are we eating inside?"

"Yes, dear," Grandma said. "It's too hot out there." She took a wine glass out of the cabinet. "Milk or juice?"

"Juice. Please."

Twilight made the big glass door in the dining room both a window and a mirror, reflecting my grandparents, sitting at opposite ends of the table, with me in between. They drank their wine and smiled at each other. I remembered how they used to talk about the work that needed doing—peas to pick and shell, cherries to pit and can, the asparagus bed to weed. I twisted my fork in spaghetti. It was good, but I wondered why we weren't having any garden vegetables.

"Have you seen any box turtles in the garden?"

"Saw one … must have been two, three weeks ago," Grandpa said. "Saw a snapper crossing the dam yesterday."

"How big?"

Grandpa tapped his plate. "This big around."

"They're digging nests now and laying eggs."

Grandma cleared her throat. "Your mom says you're doing fine in school. She says you've made a friend."

"Yeah, Cathy. She's got a dog. I think I'm allergic."

"And you have a job? After school, in a pet shop?"

"Uh-huh. They have all kinds of reptiles from around the world. They have giant pythons and lizards and frogs with red eyes. It's not really a job, though. I just like going there to help out and be with the animals."

Grandpa nudged me with his elbow. "Do you have a boyfriend?"

"No!"

"Oh, hush, John," Grandma said.

Grandpa winked at me and scooted his chair away from

the table. He stood and patted my shoulder, then took his wine into the living room and turned on the TV.

"Well," Grandma said, "I'm glad to know you are enjoying your new life in the city."

Before I could say anything, Grandma stood up and stacked the plates and carried them to the kitchen. I followed her and started drying the dishes after she washed them. When we were done, Grandma patted my backside and said, "Thank you, dear," and then went to join Grandpa in the living room.

I finished putting away the dishes and went upstairs to Spot. His eyes were shut and his arms were tucked back along his sides. I lifted him from the heat mat, tucked him in bed, pulled the covers up to his nose, and kissed him good night.

Grandpa was asleep and Grandma was reading when I got back downstairs. On the TV, *60 Minutes* was going *tick-tick-tick-tick*. I stood behind Grandma's chair, wishing she would come sit on the porch with me and listen to frogs and crickets. Then I could tell her how I was *not* enjoying my new life in the city and that I wanted to come home to Mooresville. Something felt big in my throat. I swallowed hard and went out by myself.

Pushing the door shut on cold air and TV noise, I stepped into a night alive with frog and cricket voices. The warm cement felt good on my bare feet. I saw my shadow and looked up at the sky. The cloud blanket had gone. Light from the moon made everything white glow—my shorts, the diving board, and the painted frames of the screen doors. The water's surface and the green-black ivy leaves around Grandma's sundial held a silvery shine. I could almost see the time on the sundial.

I turned and saw a luna moth sitting on the side of the house. I slid my fingers underneath her so that she had to climb onto me. Her pale green wings covered my whole hand, and the rusty-brown edges were crisp and unbroken, the wing tails long and perfect. I carried her to the diving board and sat down. I looked at her plump, furry body, her face with eyes like big poppyseeds and antennae like tiny rust-colored combs sticking up. Her wings began to tremble, but I knew she wasn't afraid. She was excited about flying around in the moonlight and finding a mate and laying eggs.

I watched the luna moth crawl up my arm. Her feet tickled and scratched like a baby lizard's. The frogs and crickets were so loud the night was ringing with their song. I looked up at the dark blue sky. With the moon so bright, the stars looked far away and they didn't twinkle, except when bats flew in front of them. I felt like I was in the center of the world, with the open sky above and the house and giant trees making a circle around me.

A bullfrog said *rrraalmph, rrraalmph, rrraalmph,* and another answered. The two bullfrogs talked to each other, back and forth, their voices so round and deep they vibrated in my chest. Cricket frogs said *click-click-click-click-click.* Spring peepers asked *reeep? reeep? reeep?* Their song always flooded me with happiness and ache all at once. I knew it would end soon, the way spring ended, and the peepers would be silent for a whole year. I wished I could stay up all night and listen to the frogs and make it all last, every minute.

The luna moth flew up, flapping wings of green moonlight, spiraling higher, getting smaller, until she disappeared in the treetops. Flashes of light came from beyond the trees like silent explosions in the distance. Grandma called it heat lightning.

The next morning I took Spot down to the pond. The water's surface was like a mirror lit up by the white-hot sky. I stood barefoot in the mud and looked at the reflection of my big, spiky-crested lizard holding on to me. His nose touched my cheek, his black-banded tail reached down to my knees, and his scales were all different shades of green. His toes fanned out against my T-shirt and his claws poked through, scratching my stomach a little. I wriggled my feet down into the warm mud, making a wet earth smell rise up. I breathed it in deep and I felt so happy I couldn't imagine ever being sad again. We were a long, long way from the city. Rings rippled our reflection as a red dragonfly touched the water's surface with her tail, releasing tiny eggs.

I saw the bullfrog over by the lagoon in the shade of leafy branches hanging over the water. His throat and its reflection made a big patch of yellow against the ring of dark mud that went around the pond, separating weeds from water. Somewhere in the distance a lawn mower buzzed. A cricket frog poked his shiny-bumpy head up out of the water to see if it was safe to go back to his place on the bank. In the woods the pileated woodpecker rattled out his wild call. Spot flicked out his tongue and I kissed his lips and we walked to the garden, making the cricket frogs plink and plop into the water.

The garden had shrunk. I could see the square patch of healthy weeds that was the ghost of the old garden. Spot leaned away from me, pushing against my arm, wanting down. I set him near the pea vines that were almost done making peas and he started eating the leaves, tugging and tearing them off the plants. The lawn-mower noise grew louder. I turned to look past the apple trees at Barney Cooke's cornfield. It wasn't a cornfield anymore, but a bright green lawn. A man was riding a tractor around a new beige house that sat in the middle of the lawn like it had dropped from the sky.

Spot had climbed over the cabbages and was going head first into the squash plants to eat the flowers. He wouldn't know the difference between the male flowers and the female ones. Grandma would be mad if he ate the female ones with the little round green fruits swelling at their bases. I held Spot back with one hand and reached in past the giant prickly-haired leaves and picked the male flowers. Just three of them filled my hand with their soft orange petals. I shook out the bees, checked for crab spiders and fed each flower to Spot. Powdery yellow pollen covered his lips. When I tried to wipe it off, he pulled away and started walking up the row between cabbages and squash plants, tasting the soil here and there, leaving behind lizard footprints with a tail drag down the middle. When he reached the edge of the garden I picked him up and set him on my shoulder to continue our walk.

Grandpa had not mowed the field. Dry grass scratched my ankles and the fuzzy seed heads of weeds tickled my legs. We walked around the pond toward the tractor path that went straight through the brambles. Grandpa hadn't actually cut a path through the thorny bushes; they had grown up over the path. Grandma once told me how the row of brambles came to be. There had been a fence to keep the horses in the field from straying into the woods.

"Birds planted it," she said. "They perched along that fence and left droppings full of seeds."

Before long—in just a few seasons—thorny branches of blackberry and wild rose shot up out of the ground and grew so tall they arched over the path to meet with the trees on the other side. Walking underneath the arched branches felt like being inside a tunnel of green. Rabbits nested at the edge of the path and raised their babies inside the tunnel, and box turtles came to eat the blackberries. The cardinal and mocking bird built nests in the thorny thickets, where the babies were protected from foxes and skunks. It was a place where I could hide, too, and pretend that I had run off to live with wild animals.

"The berries won't be ripe," I told Spot, "but you can eat the roses."

As we came to the place in the field where the tractor path was supposed to be, I stopped and looked along the edge of the woods. I thought I had gone too far, but then I saw the path, the full length of it, going all the way to the edge of the grass that surrounded the house. A whole jungle of blackberry bushes and wild roses was gone. I held on to Spot and walked up the path. Even the old fence was missing. I felt a sharp pain in my foot, and I lifted it to see. A dry thorny twig was stuck in my heel. It was the only evidence that the brambles had ever been here.

Years ago I had stood in this very place underneath the leafy ceiling and watched hover flies dance in a shaft of sunlight. I remembered how a hermit thrush would fill the brambles with his flute voice, sweet and sad all at once. It made me stand still, as though I was being held by his song. Spot flicked my cheek with his tongue and I squeezed his tail.

On the way up the path to the house Spot started jerking his head this way and that, twisting himself around and scratching to get down. I let him, to see what he wanted. He ran into the woods, his feet barely touching the ground, scattering dry leaves in his flight. He leapt onto a tree and started to climb the trunk. I saw how his long toes reached around and his claws sank into the bark, and how his tail pressed against the tree like an extra foot. He climbed higher, his spine bending side to side, and I marveled at seeing that he was made to be in the trees.

Suddenly I realized how angry my grandparents would be if we had to call the fire department to get Spot down. Standing on my tiptoes and reaching up high, I grabbed the base of his tail and pulled him off the tree, bringing down bits of lichen and bark on my face and in my eyes. Spot struggled and scratched and spun his tail around, and my arms got scratches and welts from tail slaps. When I brought him to me and held him close, he stopped. His ribs moved in and out, breathing hard, and I could hear his tongue flicking my neck to be sure where he was. After a minute I held him out to see his face. His head was pale, and some of the scales around his neck and shoulders had turned orange. With wide-open eyes he searched the treetops and then he started struggling again, pushing against me with his rough, scaly palms. I held on to him tight and hurried back to the house.

Up in my room I sat beside Spot under the basking light. His eyes were still wide open, and he stood stiff and tongue-flicked the rug. He looked up at the ceiling and at the walls, turning his head slowly, his eyes narrowing and then opening. He blinked. Then he looked at me as though studying my face. I held out a piece of banana from his dish, and he ate it. His colors were changing—his head went back to gray-green and his body's greens and blues returned. Some of the scales on his arms stayed orange. He licked his lips and settled his belly on the rug. I rested my hand on his back a while.

Later I found Grandma and Grandpa playing cards on the living room carpet. Grandma sat with her legs apart, dealing the cards, while Grandpa watched, stretched out on his side, leaning on his elbow. They looked like a couple of kids bent over a game of marbles.

"Okay, queens are up," Grandma said.

"What happened to the brambles?" I asked, sitting down cross-legged.

"Queens *up*," Grandpa said.

"Right." Grandma took the queen off the pile and put it with the others above the line of cards. "Bob Ellis took them out for us," she answered, not looking up.

"But why?"

"It was a lot of work to maintain that path, dear. Every fall we had to put on heavy gloves and cut out— "

"Ace over," Grandpa interrupted.

"Oh, yes," Grandma said, moving the ace.

"Why couldn't you just leave them?"

"Because it was becoming an overgrown mess. Let's see—we need a red four." Grandma moved through the cards in her hand, three at a time.

I shifted my legs, recrossing them. "Did Bob Ellis cut down the dead trees in the woods, too?"

"Yep. He's been a big help."

"What about the garden—how about that?"

"The garden?"

"It shrank."

"We decided not to plant so many tomatoes this year."

"Whoops," Grandpa said. "Play the jack."

"Right, right." Grandma backed up six cards and slapped the jack on the pile. "Solitaire is a two-person game," she said, laughing a little.

"But I thought you loved to garden and work outside," I said, kind of loud.

"Sure we do, but we don't want it to be a full-time job anymore." Grandma sighed heavily, stopping the game. "Dear, your grandfather and I are getting old." Finally she looked at me over her glasses. "Grace! You look as though you've been crawling through brambles."

"My heavens," Grandpa said, as if he'd just noticed me sitting there.

"Where'd you get those scratches?" Grandma asked. "And those holes in your shirt?"

"Spot got a little excited on our walk, that's all."

"You had better go clean those scratches, Grace."

"I *will*, Grandma." I brushed at the scratches. "You and Grandpa are *not* old."

"Think I'll go fiddle with the bush hog," Grandpa said. He patted my shoulder, pushed himself up off the floor, and walked out toward the garage, whistling.

Grandma shuffled the cards once and set the deck neatly on the coffee table. "Why the long face?"

"I don't like what's happening to Mooresville."

She sat, waiting.

"The only reason I did okay in school is because I could always think about Mooresville being here and the garden and woods and you and Grandpa and me coming back home."

"Well, we're here—for now, anyway. And we'll keep planting a garden, even if it's not very big. But Grace, your home is with your mother in the city."

"I don't like it there!" I could hear myself whining. If my mother were here, she would tell me to stop.

"I am sorry, dear. Though I do believe you will be just fine, even if you don't feel that way right now."

"I have to check on Spot." I got up and went upstairs, trying not to stomp. It wasn't fair, the way they decided things for me, like where I had to live and what happened to the things I loved.

Spot was napping under his light, perfectly calm. Whatever his problem was, he'd gotten over it. I sat down on the edge of my bed and looked out the window at the robin's nest in the wisteria. Downy tufts stuck up—the second batch of eggs had hatched. I didn't get up to see, though. I felt tired. But I didn't want to sleep; I didn't know what I wanted. I wished I had brought my paints and my jacket.

The spring peepers had stopped peeping long ago. I stood on my balcony and looked out at the woods. The haze in the air made the edges of the leaves look soft and blur together. Thunder rumbled in the distance the way it did every day, but there was no storm coming; it was the same old hot white sky with no clouds. In this kind of heat, turtles and water snakes would be out at the pool at the bottom of Keller Hill, where the water was always cooler than in the pond or the swimming pool.

I put on my T-shirt with the claw holes and my cutoffs. Leaving Spot asleep on my bed, I went down the stairs and out the door. The sun was a fierce ball of white light in the white sky. My hair felt damp and heavy, and the hot grass felt sticky on my feet.

After crossing the tractor path, I walked by the stable with its locked door. Grandma said they'd had Bob Ellis put the door on because of all the new traffic on Keller Hill Road. I wanted to ask Mr. Ellis, did he ever think about what the swallows felt like when they came back in the spring to build their nest and couldn't get in?

From the middle of the field I could see woods and farms and fields beyond. I saw that new house sitting in Barney Cooke's cornfield, and I didn't like the feeling it gave me—that I shouldn't be out here, going for a walk down to the creek. It was as if I was trespassing, somehow. Suddenly I didn't want to be out there, out in the open, and I ran down the hill into the trees at the edge of the field where the creek met the road.

The creek was low, but I could hear water falling into the pool on the other side and I started climbing up the bank, feeling that excitement I used to get, because whenever I visited the pool I saw something wonderful. Once I was sitting on the rock and I saw the sand on the bank move. I stared at it for a minute and a tiny black head poked up, followed by a shell the size of a quarter with a long tail out behind. More baby snapping turtles hatched and dug their way out and scuttled on tiny legs straight for the water. Crows perched up in the trees and flapped and cawed, unwilling to come down to eat the turtles with me there.

Now I had to put my hands on the new guardrail and straddle it while I brought one leg over, then the other, and again it felt like trespassing. I heard a car coming and I hurried across the road, pulled myself over the other guardrail, and climbed down the bank, holding on to roots and saplings. I looked down in time to see the tail of a water snake slip off the flat rock into the pool. As soon as I reached the bottom, I went to the rock and sat down.

Over the sound of falling water I could barely hear a car pass above. No one could see me down here. I settled in, waiting for the snake to come back. The rock was cool against the backs of my legs. Thick green moss grew where water splashed rock endlessly. The smell of the moss was sweet and earthy and I had an urge to lower my foot and touch it with my toes, but

I couldn't move if I wanted the snake to come back. I heard thunder in the distance. A green frog climbed to his place on a rock across the pool, and I began to see other frogs perched on the rocks. Silvery minnows hung in the water, their gill fins waving slowly. Ripples appeared on the surface of the pool, and the snake's head poked up, his tongue flicking in and out fast. His body went out behind in *S* waves as he pushed himself up out of the water onto the rock, inches from my feet. I held perfectly still as he glided into the patch of sunlight where he had been before. His tongue flicked in and out. He knew I was there. The snake coiled up and rested his head on his body, facing the pool. Soon his tongue quit flicking in and out.

Again, I heard thunder, closer, and a clear voice said *urrr-urrr-urrr.* It was a gray tree frog, who sings before rain. He made me think of Walter and wonder what he was doing back at Fang & Claw. If Walter were here, he could tell me the scientific name of the water snake. Then maybe we could follow the creek through the woods and look for box turtles and salamanders.

I watched the snake breathe, the brown mottled pattern on his skin moving out-in, out-in. His plump body and keeled scales made him look soft as velvet. I wanted to pet him, and I thought if I moved very slowly he might let me. But the moment I lifted my hand he slipped into the water. I reached out after him, even though he was gone. My eyes stung at the corners and I looked up at the sky, at the circle of white overhead ringed by maple and oak and sycamore leaves. I let out a breath, let my eyes follow a grapevine down the trunk of a tree, the vine getting thicker and then branching out sideways to join a tangle of vines hanging from another tree. Chameleons should be there, climbing on those vines, holding on to tendrils with mitten hands and feet. Fat boas should be coiled up resting in the crooks of branches, and great iguanas should be stretched out along the thicker vines, their long toes and tails hanging down.

I sat for a minute with my knees pulled up under my chin, staring into the water. A crawdad walked along the side of a rock, picking at algae with his claws. The water held him as if gravity didn't exist down there.

After stretching out my legs and scooting to the edge of the rock, I lowered myself into the pool all the way up to my neck. Then I put my head under so the water covered me completely.

As I climbed up to the road, my wet hair and clothes felt cool and good against my skin. I should be happy—I had been sitting with a snake beside a waterfall, unbothered, watching frogs and crawdads. But I was sad and didn't know why.

Crossing the road I popped a tar bubble with my big toe and told myself to remember to clean that off before walking on Grandma's carpet. I was about to climb over the other guard-rail when I heard a truck. It sounded like Barney Cooke's old Ford. When it came speeding over the hill, I saw that it was an old Ford, but not Barney's. There were kids in the truck, older ones, boys and girls. Orange and yellow beach towels flapped and arms waved and I raised my hand to wave back.

As the truck passed, I saw wide eyes and open mouths and fingers pointing at me. One of the boys stood and his hands went up to his chest like something was there, and I gasped and covered myself with my arms. The horn blared, making me jump. My heart pounded and the Ford sped away with four kids in bathing suits who were sitting on inner tubes and looking back at me. I picked up a rock and threw it after them and watched it bounce along the pavement and roll to a stop in the middle of the road.

I looked down at myself, sticking out, with the soaking wet T-shirt full of holes, clinging to my skin, showing everything.

A chainsaw buzzed in the distance. I made it over the guardrail and down to the creek bed, and then I ran with my arms crossed in front, stumbling over rocks and tree roots. I kept to the woods as long as I could, but finally I had to run across the lawn to the house.

My grandma called, "Grace?" but I didn't answer. Upstairs I turned on the bathroom light and looked in the mirror. Why didn't I see before? Nobody told me; they just let me go around like that. I wanted to smash the mirror with my fists. I pushed open my bedroom door, grabbed a shirt off a hanger, and wrapped it around myself. I lay down on the bed next to Spot and pulled him close and hid my face in the folds of his dewlap.

"It is time for us to go to town and shop for school clothes," my grandmother said.

I used to like trying on dresses and bright sweaters and

coveralls that my grandma picked out and brought to the fitting room. But now I didn't want to take off my clothes when it was time to. I stood in my underwear and shivered, even though the fitting room was hot and stuffy. Grandma brought a saleslady to the room. The saleslady had a tight mouth and hair all stiff and sprayed.

"Grace," Grandma said, "the lady needs to see you so she can bring a size to try on, dear."

I took my arms away from my chest. The saleslady looked at me and said, "Huh," and left. Grandma followed. I covered myself again and looked at the floor. I didn't want to see myself in the dressing room mirrors.

When the saleslady came back she handed me a white bra to try on. I stared at the straps and hooks.

"You put your arms through the straps," the saleslady said, as if I was dumb.

I put on the bra and turned around for my grandma to hook the back. She patted the strap and said, "The B cup fits. Just." Grandma smiled at me in the mirror. "She's growing fast, though. We'd better take a C."

Grandma bought me a couple of shirts and a skirt that I could wear to school, and she got me a two-piece bathing suit, too, a green one with a leaf pattern that I liked. But when I got home and dove into the pool in my new suit, I missed my shorts—they'd always stayed on. The top part of the new swimsuit got pushed down and sideways, and the bottoms went around my knees.

—

The gray tree frog at the pool had been right about rain coming. For two days it poured. The creek filled up and the pond was muddied with all the water flowing in. The clear air and blue sky of late summer in Mooresville had come. I dragged a bench by the pool, put down a towel, and stretched out on my back in the sun.

I felt tired and wanted to sleep, but I couldn't lie still. I got up and started walking around the pool ledge, careful not to step on ants or spiders. Tiny cracks ran through the cement and I stepped between them and over the grout lines in a sort of aimless hopscotch. Looking at my feet, I thought about how Cathy had wanted to paint my toenails dragon red. I kicked a pebble across the patio. I had to keep reaching back to tug on the elastic of my swimsuit bottoms.

I heard Grandpa's tractor. The whirring of the bush hog grew louder and the red tractor came around the side of the house. Grandpa had on a long-sleeved shirt and a hat, because the doctor said he needed to cover up when he worked in the sun. I waved, but he didn't see me. Bits of grass blew across the edge of the patio as the tractor passed by. Sweat soaked the back of Grandpa's shirt. I went inside to fix a jar of ice water for him.

Carrying the water across the yard, I watched Grandpa's face. He saw me and pushed pedals and levers, stopping the tractor but not the engine. Its hot wind blew against my legs and stomach. I held the jar up to Grandpa and he took it and drank, spilling water down his shirt. He gave me back the jar with only ice left in it. Then he reached over and patted my shoulder.

"Thank you, sweetheart," he said. "Watch out, now."

My grandfather pulled the lever and dropped the bush hog. I stepped back. He took his foot off the brake and the tractor jerked forward, leaving behind a wide path of cut grass.

I walked up to the house, went inside, and dumped the ice in the laundry room sink. I felt like throwing the jar on the floor. Instead, I set it down in the sink with the melting ice and went to find my grandma. She was asleep in her chair in the living room, with glasses halfway down her nose, a book open on her lap. The quiet, air-conditioned house gave me goose bumps. I went back outside.

Squinting in the bright light, I stood and looked around, trying to figure out what to do. The grass and trees were a deep, late-summer green. Mooresville should have been a jungle by now, overgrown with wild rose and blackberry bushes, their long, thorny branches reaching out in all directions. The woods should have been thick with snags and fallen branches and vines growing on them. Bob Ellis had cut every stray twig and shoot. Dead branches had been gathered and burned. I wondered where the woodpeckers would find food when winter came.

I started walking, away from the sound of the tractor and from my sleeping grandmother. Soon I would have to go back to the city. I felt stuck, not wanting to go, not wanting to be where I was. I didn't know where I could go and be okay. I walked, not caring which way I went, watching the lines of my swimsuit blur into the grass until I saw that I had come down the path where the brambles used to be. I stopped and held a tear between my eyelashes. It was like peering through a tiny prism. For a second I was back in the tunnel of green light, the way it used to be before Bob Ellis cut away the brambles. I squeezed out the tear and saw the snake, right there at the edge of the path.

His neck was curved, because he had seen me and was being careful about coming out of the tall weeds. He held his head up, watching me, but I could tell that he wasn't afraid. I knelt close to him and he didn't run away. His red and black tongue flicked in and out. His eye moved, a black pupil inside a gold ring. He let me reach underneath his chin and touch his glossy throat. I pulled my hand away slowly and kept still and watched his sides move in and out with each breath.

Soon he came out of the weeds. His brown-and-cream-striped ribbon body made S shapes across the path. He didn't hurry. I wondered where he was going and what he wanted. He flicked his tongue in and out as he went, checking what was in front of him, and then he entered the weeds on the other side of the path. I watched him go, watched the dark tip of his tail slip away, and I caught my breath. I stayed like that, squatting in the path, looking at where the snake had been. After a while I stood up and walked back to the house, back to Spot.

I thought about how I had been walking around Mooresville barefoot with a big lizard for my companion, as though we were creatures of the forest. But Spot was from a tropical forest far away. He was an outsider, and so was I.

Spot opened his eyes and looked at me. I gathered him in my arms and kissed his nose, his chin, the side of his face, and all down his neck and shoulders. I couldn't stop. He tongue-flicked my ear and I rested my cheek on his side. His claws holding on to my shoulder and my ribs made me feel better. He didn't struggle to get down the way he did when he wanted to climb the tree, and he didn't shut his eyes the way he did when he was tired of something.

We went out to bask on the ledge by the pool. Grandma's flowerbed blazed with red, orange, and yellow nasturtiums that needed picking so more buds would open. Leaving Spot beside the pool, I gathered the blossoms, stuffing them between my cupped hand and my stomach. When I had all I could hold, I carried the flowers back to Spot and let them spill over my lap. I held a red one out to Spot, and he ate it. I ate one, too. It tasted sweet and peppery. One after another I fed Spot the flowers and watched his sticky tongue pull each one into his jaws.

When all the flowers were gone, Spot spread his belly on the warm cement. I did the same. We faced each other, nose to nose. He put his arms back along his sides. So did I. He pushed out his dewlap to catch the sun. After a while our skin darkened. Mine tanned brown; his was like rust on lava rock. Heat rising off the cement made the edges of the patio look quivery. I imagined lizards everywhere, darting in and out of cracks and basking on the ledge. Spot looked at me and bobbed his head up and down, as though trying to tell me something.

After a while Spot opened his mouth to cool himself. I could see the thick pink muscles inside and the small triangle-shaped teeth lining his jaws. Moments later he leaned toward the water and slipped in. I followed and dove down below. When I saw his shadow on the pool floor I turned over and looked up. He swam like a crocodile, his arms and legs back along his sides and tail, curving side to side slowly across the water's surface. Fingers of sunlight shimmered around him and down through the water. The shadow of his tail moved across my eyes, and I breathed out a bubble that looked like a jellyfish rising.

I wanted to stay down there suspended in the calm, clear water. I stayed down as long as I could, until my chest hurt and I had to push off the bottom with my feet and go up for air. Spot was sitting on the ledge again, looking down at me through the water. I climbed out and sat beside him.

New York City

The subway car stank of vomit. Everything stank; it was all too much. Spot had bitten me. I didn't know what I had done wrong, but I had to stop thinking about it or I would turn into a dumb crybaby again. I'd been doing that a lot lately. Like on Saturday at the airport, when I saw this father meeting his daughter. He gave her a great big hug and then held her back at arm's length.

"Why, you've blossomed into a young woman," he told her.

I felt sick. I watched the girl blush and smile as if what he'd said made her happy. And then he hugged her again. I had to find the bathroom and splash water on my face. No one would ever use that word to describe what was happening to me. What was happening to me had nothing to do with flowers. When I looked up at the mirror I saw another pimple on my forehead. I couldn't stop the tears. It was like first grade again, washing my face in the girls' bathroom a lot because I kept getting homesick.

The train screeched to a stop and the doors clattered open. I climbed out of the subway station and walked to school. It was miserably hot, and I was sweating in the old work shirt I'd taken from my grandfather's closet. It was all I had to wear. My favorite T-shirt with Spot's claw holes didn't fit anymore, because my horrible chest had stretched it. And I'd looked at the nice new clothes Grandma had bought for me, but I couldn't bear to wear them now.

Upstairs on the fourth floor the same group of boys from middle school stood around the lockers. They had grown over the summer, but I was still taller. I had to walk past them to get to my locker.

One said, "Grace grew up."

"You mean out," said another.

They giggled like idiots. I gripped the dial on the combination lock. With them watching, it was hard to get the numbers right. Finally I got it open, put my books inside, and slammed the door shut. They giggled some more.

At lunchtime I went to the library and sat in one of the carrels behind the bookshelves. After a while Cathy came up behind me and wrapped her arms around my shoulders. "Hey, you!"

"Hi, Cathy." I reached up and squeezed her wrist.

"What are you doing here? Everyone's down in the cafeteria." She came around and sat down on the floor with her back against a bookshelf. "Whoa, you grew curves."

I glared at her. She'd changed over the summer, too—only she'd gotten prettier.

"Ooo, somebody's on the rag."

"Do you have to say it so loud?"

"Grace, there's no one in here. Anyway, what's the big deal? Join the club."

"Spot bit me."

"Damn, I bet that hurt! Do you know why?"

I shook my head. But just then I knew. It was about the blood.

"You must have startled him. Maybe he didn't recognize you. Grace?"

"Sorry."

"I bet he's stressed out about being on an airplane. It'll pass."

"Sure."

"Listen," she said, tucking her hair behind her ears, "I met this guy, Dan? He goes to NYU, do you believe it? He's only seventeen, but he's so smart they put him in college a year early. He's a physics major, and God is he cute! Not only that, he knows all these cool places to eat in the Village. We went out every weekend. I swear I had the best summer."

Cathy sat up straight, her green eyes wide open, talking the way she always did, but there was a calm about her even though she was excited.

"Grace," she said, "we've gotta find you a guy. Then the four of us can go out together."

I just looked at her.

"And what's with the shirt?"

"It's my grandfather's gardening shirt."

"You should have left it in the garden."

After school I went home to see Spot. I climbed the ladder and sat down in front of his cage. From his branch he watched me with wide-open eyes, as if I was the enemy. His scales glowed orange with whatever it was that had turned him into a beast, and he bobbed his big head up and down and flapped his swollen jowls. His dewlap was pushed out as far as it would go. A bruise ringed his nose from when he'd tried to force it through the chicken wire. I felt terrible—he was hurting and he wanted out so bad.

I held blueberries in my hand. His gold lizard eye followed my other hand as I opened the cage door. The round black pupil dilated. I reached in cautiously—his teeth were sharp. He bobbed his head some more, ignoring the berries. I put them in his dish, then slowly reached up and put my hand on him. His jowls swelled under my touch. He turned his head, tongue-flicking my skin again and again, and then he opened his jaws and leaned toward my hand. I pulled away and shut the cage door. He had slept beside me every night for so long. My throat closed up. I looked at him with tears running down my face, and he bobbed his head at me furiously.

Spot's teeth had cut into my leg like knives the night before. I tried to pry him off, but his claws dug in and his scales scraped my skin raw. When he finally let go I threw back the sheet. In gray morning light I saw that the scales had turned orange around his head and shoulders. His eyes were wild and wide open, and he stood with his tail arched. He licked blood from his lips, making the soft clicking sound he always made when he cleaned his teeth.

Pressing a sock against the bite, I hurried to the bathroom to splash peroxide on the V-shaped wounds. Pink bubbly streaks ran down my leg. In the mirror I saw my body with its swellings and blemishes and dark hair beginning to grow in places. That was when I saw the other blood.

After school the next day I took the train to Fourteenth Street. I stood against the doors with my backpack over my shoulder, nervously picking at a tear in the edge of my shirt. When Walter saw me he would be disgusted and not want me around, or he would laugh the way the boys at school did. I kept telling myself that Walter wasn't like them, but I was still scared. Then there was the problem with Spot. How was I supposed to talk about that?

When I saw the Fang & Claw sign my stomach quivered. The light changed and I crossed the street. Remembering to breathe, I pushed open the gate and went inside, and there was Walter in his Bronx Zoo T-shirt with Sue around his shoulders.

"Grace! You're back." He smiled, and I couldn't help it—I smiled too.

"Hi, Walter." I put my hands in my pockets. When I did that, my shirt hung more like a tent.

"We missed you. Wait till you see the baby *Ceratophrys*. They're taking mouse limbs and their tails are all but gone. Help me put Sue back and I'll show you."

He hadn't really seen me yet. I followed him around to where the big snake cases were.

"You won't be much help with your hands in your pockets," he said, lifting Sue's thick body from his shoulders.

I unhooked the case latch and held up the top while Walter settled Sue down inside.

"Thanks, I've got it now." He lowered the top and latched it shut.

I kept waiting for him to finally notice and cover his mouth to hide the smirk, or the other thing I got lately—the trying-not-to-look look.

"Come see the frogs," he said.

In the back room he showed me a tray lined with plastic

cups. In each cup, in a tiny bit of water, sat a frog the size of a fat grape. Nearly all mouth and eyes, each one was a miniature copy of his or her parents, with splotches of green and brown, and little legs and toes and a nub where a tail had been.

Walter took my hand and then he lifted one of the cups and tipped it so the baby frog slid into my palm. He was a wet little ball of life. I brought him closer to see, but not too close, because I didn't want him to feel my breath and be afraid that I might eat him. He looked up at me, his throat pulsing rapidly.

"Did you ever see anything so cute?" Walter asked. Just then the baby frog wiped his eye with a foot. "Last time you were here he was a dot in a cluster of eggs."

The frog began to wriggle around in my hand and his throat pulsed faster. "He's getting too warm, I think."

Walter put fresh water in the cup and held it while I put the frog in. "We're heading into breeding season, which means that some of us won't eat and some of us are hungry all the time. I was about to feed Sue."

"Let me help." I rolled up my sleeves.

Walter killed the rat and I held up the top of Sue's case and we watched her take her meal.

"Who's the other Burmese?"

"Albert, from the case up there. We brought him down because we're putting him in with her when the weather turns cool."

"He's the biggest snake I've ever seen."

"Badmouth is twice as big. Do you want to see him?"

"Yeah, I'd love to."

"Great! Let's go when Pops comes back."

We fed the geckos and anoles and got the frogs misted before I heard the gate creak and the rustle of plastic bags. Pops walked in with greens for the tortoises.

"Why, there's the lovely Grace."

I put my hands in my pockets. "Hi, Pops," I said.

"Dad, we're going over to see Badmouth. The small lizards are done and Sue is fed, okay?"

"All righty, then," Pops said.

Pushing the gate open, Walter motioned for me to go first. That felt funny, but then we were walking side by side and it was nice.

"I hope you like Badmouth," he said.

"Of course I will."

"Well, it's kind of a shock the first time you see all those teeth. I remember how horrified I was when I first saw him—not because of the teeth, actually, but because of the condition of his mouth. You wouldn't want to see that. But now the wounds have healed and he's got loads of charm. To me, anyway." Walter stopped in front of a brick building five stories high. "This is it."

We climbed the stairs to the top floor. The doorframes to the apartments and the hand railing had so much brown paint on them they looked like they'd been dipped in chocolate. Walter took out his keys, unlocked the door, and pushed it open. Inside the apartment it was so bright and sunny I had to rub my eyes after being in the dark stairs. Sunlight streamed in through four tall windows. A breakfast table and chairs stood by the kitchen window, and on the table was a teapot and two cups. I looked at them and felt something like longing, but I didn't know what for.

Spider plants and thick ferns in baskets hung from hooks in the ceiling, and potted philodendrons sat on pedestals with their leafy vines hanging down to the floor. "I wish my room was like this, like a beautiful forest," I said.

Walter hung his coat over the back of the couch, and then he took mine and put it there, too. "I never had a friend up before."

Violet-tinged light filled the room. There wasn't much furniture, only the couch and a coffee table stacked with nature books and *National Geographic* magazines. Against one wall stood a shelf with tanks that might or might not have been occupied. Inside each tank was a hide box on plain brown paper and a water bowl.

"Those are for animals in quarantine," Walter said.

Two doors faced each other down a short hallway.

"That's my dad's room. And this one's mine. It's pretty empty." He opened the door. "I gave up having anything breakable when Badmouth moved in."

Walter's room was green with leaves, like the living room, but all the plants hung from the ceiling, except for an avocado tree so big it could not have fit through the door. Its broad leaves touched the ceiling.

"How did you get the tree in?"

"I started it from a pit in the first grade."

Under the tree was a desk and chair. The desktop was bare;

books and papers were stacked on the floor. On the walls were posters—a phylogenetic tree of the snakes, a big, glossy one of velociraptors from *Jurassic Park*, and a map of Indonesia, where reticulated pythons came from. Pushed against the wall was a mattress on the floor, and next to that, a wooden case. Half the front was glass and the other half was a wooden panel. It wasn't much larger than the cases at Fang & Claw, so I thought Walter might have exaggerated about how big Badmouth was.

Walter knelt in front of the case and opened the wooden panel. It opened down, like a drawbridge. He sat back on his knees. "I never go in after him. But he'll come out, he always does. He's got to be curious about you."

Then a great, tawny-scaled head appeared, gray-eyed and with a tongue flicking in and out fast. His cat's-eye pupils moved, and sure enough, his teeth showed like a snarling dog's with lips pulled back. Except that Badmouth had more teeth, long and curved and a lot sharper than a dog's.

"They say retics are mean, but it's not true. They're smart, and smart animals expect to be treated with kindness."

Badmouth came out of his case and slid into Walter's arms, his tongue flicking slowly now, touching here and there. Walter hadn't exaggerated. He took the python's head in both hands.

"How could you not love a face like this?"

I saw that Walter and the snake had eyes the same color gray. Badmouth was rising from Walter's arms, pulling toward me. I stood still.

"You want to take his head?"

I held out both hands and Badmouth came to me, flicking

my skin with his tongue. I couldn't take my eyes off the teeth. Scar tissue had covered over the heat-sensing pits on his upper jaw, and his nostrils were all but closed off. More of his great body moved into my arms and I could feel the muscles working underneath his glassy belly scales.

"Why don't we sit," Walter said. Holding on to Badmouth's lower half he turned around to sit on the edge of the mattress. Badmouth shifted his weight suddenly, pulling against me, and I lost my balance and sat down hard on the bed with the big snake in my lap.

"Oh, sorry!" I lifted Badmouth's head and he flicked out his tongue between all those teeth. "Did I hurt you?"

"Don't worry, he's fine. You can see why the bed is on the floor."

"He didn't feel that heavy, not at first."

"Yeah, I know. He's only a hundred pounds, but it's mostly muscle and he knows how to use it. Let's move together this time."

We scooted back to lean against the wall, with our feet hanging off the edge of the bed and the python across our legs. I loved the weight of him. I traced the zigzag pattern with my finger and imagined painting him on my jacket. To get the iridescent colors over the top of the pattern I could paint thin lines of metallic green and turquoise over the black.

Badmouth began to move toward the edge of the bed, then onto the floor, heading straight for the desk.

"He loves that desk. Sometimes he climbs on top, sometimes he coils up underneath," Walter said.

"How do you get him back in the case?"

"He goes on his own."

"Then why have a case at all?"

"He needs his own place, where he can feel safe, where no one will bother him, not even me."

But Badmouth went around the desk and kept going, moving faster, as if he might circle the room, going round and round. "What's he doing?" I asked.

"Lately he's been restless."

"Do you know why?"

"Badmouth is in his third year."

I sat up straight. I knew what Walter was going to say, and I knew suddenly that that was Spot's problem, too. Walter blew out his breath and folded his arms across his chest.

"Last week he refused food for the first time ever. I'm in denial about it. I'll have to take care of it sooner or later, though. Probably sooner."

"Yeah?"

Walter watched his python, who was definitely searching.

"Female retics can reach lengths over twenty-five feet and weigh three hundred pounds. Can you imagine? I'll end up sleeping on the couch."

Badmouth made his way around the room, flicking his tongue and moving like a millipede, but with no legs.

"Meanwhile," Walter said, "I'll need to give him plenty of respect during the next months. The hard part will be discouraging him from sleeping beside me. I can't be kicking him in my sleep. He knows I'm male, and even though he knows I'm not a snake, I can't have him getting confused about any of that." Walter held out his hand to Badmouth, who was making his way around to us. "I haven't known retics to react to human pheromones, but there's always the possibility. In the case of certain lizards, the male will definitely respond to human pheromones."

We looked at each other. "Spot bit me," I said.

"Did he snap, or sort of latch on?"

"He latched on, all right, and wouldn't let go."

"That's a love bite. It's the best way I can explain it. Spot sees you as his mate."

"I thought he hated me, because—I don't know."

"He doesn't hate you. But we've got to find a female of his own kind, or else he'll go on biting you every mating season. It lasts four or five months."

Cathy said, "I've got a surprise."

We were sitting in the coffee shop around the corner from school, drinking cappuccinos.

"Nick Meyers asked me if you were going out with anyone!" Her eyes were bulging. The coffee made her hyper. "I can't believe you're still wearing that shirt. Anyway, I said no, and I told him to meet us here."

"Who?"

"Grace, the new guy. The junior?"

I frowned. She meant that wrestling-team guy with the buzz cut and the muscles. "No."

"Come on, it's not like I'm asking you to get married. Give him a chance."

"Why?"

"Because it would be good for you. You need to get out of the slump you're in. I mean, really, he thinks you're hot."

" 'Hot'! What is 'hot,' Cathy? I don't *want* hot!"

"Calm down. I'll rephrase it: easy on the eyes. Like it or not, you are now in the upper school and you've got curves."

"Don't forget the zits."

Cathy didn't hear me; she was waving at somebody outside. "Here he comes!"

He'd seen us and came running across the street like some athlete trying out for the track team.

"Cute, isn't he?"

I rolled my eyes. "If you say so." It had happened so fast, all in one summer, Cathy's fever about boys and that mascara she'd started wearing.

Nick Meyers appeared at our table, all ruddy-cheeked and eager. "Hey there," he said, pulling up a chair.

"Nick, this is Grace."

"Hi!" I said, trying to be nice.

"Cathy tells me you're into lizards," Nick said. He had these annoying blue eyes and he was nearly bursting out of his shirt. It was a long-sleeved T-shirt tucked in at the waist, so tight he might as well have been wearing nothing.

"That's right," I said.

"She said you're hard to get to know, but you have a good heart."

I slumped in my chair. "I'm just not good company right now."

"Oh, hey, that's fine," he said, nodding and smiling. He smiled a lot, which made me feel tired.

"You know, I've really got a lot of homework," I said, wadding up my napkin and stuffing it in my cup.

"Hey, no problem. It's great that you're committed to school."

"She has the whole weekend," Cathy said. "So, Nick, you're on the wrestling team?"

"Yeah. Last season I was tournament champion at Packer."

"And you're taking biology, right? Grace is into biology."

"Right," he said, nodding and smiling at me some more. "You're in the AP class," he said. "You should join the bio club."

"I can't. Most days I work after school."

Cathy acted surprised. "You do?"

"Cathy, Fang & Claw?"

"I thought you went there for fun."

"Listen," Nick said, "there's a tournament next Friday. Maybe afterward we could all go out."

I felt Cathy's foot pressing mine. "I can't make it." I narrowed my eyes at her. "And I really need to get home."

"Okay. Maybe some other time."

He was unflappable and so polite that when he stood up at the same time I did, I thought he was going to try to walk me to the train station. I ran out of there.

I could feel Spot watching me paint my jacket. He sat up on his branch, basking, glowing orange. Now and then our eyes met and he bobbed his head at me. I hated that he had to sleep in his cage at night, with only a heating pad to keep him warm. During the day I could hold him in my lap for a while and pet him, since I'd learned to see a bite coming. It began with lots of tongue flicking and swelling of jowls, and pretty soon he would lean toward me with open jaws and try to get a grip on my arm. At that point I'd reach up under his chest and push him back gently. He'd get a confused look in his eyes as if to say, *What did I do?* I wished I could help him.

My painting of Badmouth was almost done. But I had used all the black paint doing the zigzag pattern and I needed more to finish. Leaving my jacket on the bed to dry, I put on my sweatshirt, shut my door to keep Freda off the wet paint, and went out.

The art-supply store was ten blocks away. Cathy had called earlier to let me know that she was busy today—like most Saturdays, now that she had a boyfriend—but that I wasn't getting off the hook about Nick. I wished Cathy would forget it and we could keep doing stuff, just the two of us. I liked sitting in coffee shops with her, listening to her stories, but I didn't want to be part of them.

I stopped to wait for a traffic light and heard a loud *pssst!* that made me jump. I turned around. Two men stood outside a corner deli, leering at me. I glared at them. One of them said, "Smile, honey," and they both grinned.

My face went hot and I turned away, ready to run. Cars kept going by and the light wouldn't change and I was stuck. Finally the traffic stopped, but then all I could do was walk across the street with heavy legs. A squeaky kissing noise followed me. I wanted to turn and run at them, snarling with sharp teeth to make their grins disappear. I went around the corner to get out of sight. My fists and teeth clenched, I was so angry, and my eyes filled up and stung, because there wasn't anything I could do about what I was.

Then I saw the snake in the window. He lay still in a loose coil inside a dirty tank. It took me a second to figure out that he was a baby reticulated python, because his skin wasn't reticulated anymore. A lot of it was gone. Patches of pink, scaleless flesh broke the zigzag pattern the length of his body. I shuddered when the python's ribs moved and I knew that he was alive. The naked places looked slimy. In the corner, the mouse that must have gnawed on the snake had been dead for so long he looked like beef jerky with white tufts of fur clinging. I put my hand on the window and watched the baby python with his pushed-up nose. His eyes were dark orange, not gray like Badmouth's, and his cat's-eye pupils were narrowed to slits.

I had only a few dollars in my pocket, but I had to take the snake home. I went inside.

The pet shop smelled like a cat box. Fish tanks bubbled, and I could hear water running somewhere in the back and a clanking noise like a metal sink.

"Anyone there?" I said.

No answer. I stood in front of the snake's tank and thought about reaching in and taking him. The water stopped running in the back. A man with rolled-up sleeves carrying an empty tank appeared.

"Can I help you?" he asked impatiently.

"I'd like to see the python."

The man frowned, set the tank on the counter, and came over and took off the screen. He stood there with it hanging from one hand while he ran the other through his sweaty hair.

I reached in and lifted the snake. He felt like a section of garden hose full of ice water, slowly wrapping around my hand. Bits of gravel stuck to the skinless places, so I had to hold him carefully. Then I saw that he was a she.

"She's in bad shape," I said, bringing the snake to me. She flicked out her tongue, touching my fingers.

"Yeah, it won't eat."

"Yes, because she's *cold*. This is a tropical species—"

"Look, it's just me here, I don't have any help and I don't have time for sick animals."

"I do."

"Great. Fifty bucks."

The python had found the cuff of my sleeve, and she pushed against my hands and went in.

"I don't have that much, and anyway, have you noticed that half her skin is missing?"

I felt the snake's belly scales ripple to move her body up my arm. The man made an exasperated noise as he watched her tail disappear.

"I don't have time for this. How much do you have?"

I showed him the few crumpled bills from my pocket.

The python had wrapped around me, underneath my shirt.

I imagined the police trying to get her away from me. Maybe the pet shop man thought the same thing, because he threw his hands in the air like he was shooing flies.

"All right, take it. Give me the money and go."

"Right," I said, and walked out the door.

Trying hard not to jostle Python, I walked as fast as I could. I felt her chilled body and the raw places and I worried that my salty skin would burn them, but I held her close until we were safely home.

After filling the bathtub with warm water I unbuttoned my shirt, pulled my arms from the sleeves, and began to unwrap Python's long, skinny body from mine. I held my breath the whole time, cringing, afraid of hurting the raw flesh and of causing her to lose more skin. Finally I drew her clear and lowered her into the bath. She gulped water, chewing, like she was starving for it. Then she began to swim, making S shapes in the water while bits of mouse fur and gravel fell off the wounds. Leaving her to soak, I went to my room, pulled out a drawer, and dumped out the clothes. I put a paper bag on the bottom and a cardboard box with a hole cut in the side for an entry.

Python had passed some chalky uric acid in the water and the smallest bit of brown matter. I broke it apart, looking for blood, but didn't find any. I patted her dry in a clean dishcloth and used a whole tube of antibiotic salve to cover the wounds. She didn't snap at me once.

When I set her down near the hide box entry she went right in, leaving salve smudges on the brown paper. Coils formed, settling and pulling back from sight. I took the screen from my window, set it on top of the drawer, and weighed down the corners with books. Then I put a red heat bulb in a lamp and turned it on.

I took the train to Walter's and pushed the buzzer. As soon as he opened the door I started talking about Python. He ran back up to get a coat and the keys to the shop.

"It sounds bad," he said. He started killing mice quickly and putting them in a plastic bag. "I just hope we can get her to eat." He tucked the bag of mice inside his coat and put his forceps in his back pocket.

After locking up we hurried across Fourteenth Street and down the steps into the subway station and caught the train. It was crowded with tourists and college students going downtown to shop or to hang out in the Village.

"It's only three stops," I said.

The doors shut and the train started moving through the tunnel. We stood facing each other, both of us holding on to the pole with one hand. His fingers were white next to mine. I could feel my forehead creased with worry over Python, and I glanced up at Walter. He looked at me with his gray eyes and patted his coat where the bag of mice was. I looked away, down at my sneakers, and then wondered why I did that.

The train lurched to a stop, and we moved aside to let people go around us. Two girls got on and stood nearby, looking happy and pretty in their sweaters and slim-fitting jeans. I looked at my sneakers again, and at Walter's. His hand had slid down the pole so close my fingers tingled. I could tell that he was looking at me. It wasn't fair, the way other girls had bodies that were normal while I was stuck with a huge chest that had to be covered up with baggy clothes. I could feel my face heating up and my eyes starting to sting. It was a short ride, but it felt longer today.

Finally we got there. "This is our stop," I told Walter.

We made our way out of the subway station and hurried around people on the sidewalk. I had the keys out a block before we reached the building.

Walter gasped when he saw Python halfway out of her hide box. He got down on his knees beside her. I did too.

"Is the rest of her like this?"

"Yes."

"I never saw mouse bites this bad before," he said, pulling his arms from the sleeves of his coat. "But the worst is the way the skin is just gone in so many places."

"She was on wet gravel with no heat source."

"Yeah, well, she's in good hands now."

Walter's eyes were fierce, watching Python. She pulled back inside her box when I started moving the books off the top. I lifted the screen while Walter opened the bag of mice. The tip of Python's nose appeared at the hide box entry and her tongue flicked out. Then in his usual way—in one deft motion—Walter pulled the forceps from his pocket, took the mouse by the scruff, and offered the food to the snake. She snatched the mouse.

"Bingo!" Walter said, leaning back on his heels. I laughed and Walter nudged me with his elbow. "She'll be fine," he said.

After only a minute, Python poked her nose out and flicked her tongue in and out.

"That was fast," I said.

"Oh, sure. A mouse isn't a big meal for a baby retic."

Walter gave her another mouse, and another. After swallowing the fourth, Python waited, watching us from just outside her box. Then she yawned so wide I could have put my palm flat against her open mouth. As she stretched and moved her jaws I could see the muscles and bluish veins inside, and the windpipe and the place where her tongue came out. I could see the rows of hooked teeth nestled in the pink flesh of her mouth.

"She'll eat a lot over the next weeks and months, and she'll go into a hyper-shed until the skin heals."

"What else should I do?"

"You're doing it. Keep her warm and clean and dry, and keep the food coming."

I set the screen over the drawer and stacked the books on top. Walter took a few more books off the shelf and added them.

"I'll bring down a case from the shop. Books won't keep her in for long."

When I'd finished the painting of Badmouth I wore the jacket to school. Somehow I imagined that I'd be left alone with the big snake on my back with all those teeth showing. But when I walked into the student lounge, one of the guys gave me a nasty grin.

"Hey, Grace. Take a look at this."

They leaned against the wall, a little gang of three, pink-faced and stifling giggles. On the message board in thick red marker lines was a stick figure, the tiny head drawn above two enormous circles with details like they had really seen me. *Chester* was printed in big letters underneath the drawing.

They took off down the hall, yelling, "Chester, Chester!"

I went after them, but my chest bounced when I ran, so I stopped. They ducked into the stairwell at the end of the hall, giggling wildly. If only I could drop on all fours, sprout claws and fangs, and chase them down like rats.

Teeth clenched, I went back and smeared the message board with my bare hands. Right then I saw Nick, watching me. I looked at my hands, red from the ink, and I wiped them on the back of my jeans.

"Boys," he said. "So immature."

"It's not funny."

"Oh, I didn't think it was." Nick gave me a sincere look, his annoying blue eyes large with concern. His muscles bulged, stretching the thick material of his wrestling-team sweatshirt. "Listen, I'm heading over to the bio lab. Why don't you come along? We could help each other prep for the exams."

"I can't." No way could I stand at the lab bench beside Nick in his sweaty sweats.

"Some other time?"

"I don't know."

He smiled. "Catch you later, then."

I went to my locker, stuffed some books in my backpack, and left the school building.

The train was crowded, but I managed to find a seat in the corner. Feeling worn out and jumpy all at once, I shut my eyes. Even though I was tired I couldn't wait to be at Fang & Claw. Maybe I could just feed the small lizards, or stand at the sink and wash whatever Walter brought to me. Nick without a shirt on appeared in my head, all sweaty and flesh-colored, and I shuddered and shook my head. I felt my face in a grimace and opened my eyes.

Across the aisle a man sat looking at me in a way I didn't like. A hot spike of rage flared inside me and I glowered at the man, but he kept looking. My heart pounded. I was stuck to my seat, trapped, with the train in that long stretch between Brooklyn and Manhattan. I looked around at the other passengers and realized that nobody saw—they were all reading newspapers or sleeping. What would they do anyway?

I tried to shout, *Leave me alone!* but all that came out was a pathetic little noise. I had to grit my teeth to keep from crying.

Finally the train reached the station, and I was up out of my seat and out the doors as soon as they opened. I ran across the platform, up the stairs, and out through the turnstile. Out of breath, I stood on the corner and saw that I was way downtown, maybe twenty blocks from home and many more from Fang & Claw. I started walking as fast as I could, and when I reached my street I took out my keys, turned up the block, and went home.

Exhausted, I dropped my backpack on the floor and sat down in a chair. My head hurt and I wanted to go to bed, but I couldn't move. The telephone rang and I picked it up.

"Grace? It's Walter."

"Hi."

"I have something for you—a friend for Spot, really, and I was hoping I could come over."

I jumped up from the chair. "Okay, come on over."

When the door buzzer sounded I went out the door and halfway down the stairs. Walter came up, his coat bulging out front.

"You got here fast."

"I took a cab."

"Where did you find her?"

"I answered an ad in the *Times*. The owner said she was getting too big to take care of."

Walter unbuttoned his coat and I helped him get it off while he kept one hand on the bulge under his sweater. Finally Walter lifted the sweater and a long banded tail came out. Clinging to his shirt was a bright green iguana as big as Spot. She turned her head and looked right at me with pale gold eyes that were lit up from inside.

"Let's introduce them," Walter said.

He disengaged her claws from his shirt and gave her to me. She was warm from being inside his coat and she had the faintest smell of him on her.

Holding the lizard against my shoulder, I went up the ladder. Walter followed. I sat down on the bed with her in my lap. On hands and knees Walter went to Spot's cage and opened the door, and then he sat down cross-legged.

Spot bobbed his head right away, and the female lizard saw him too. Her eyes grew wide; so did his. They held still. Even their ribs did not move in and out; only the pupils in their wide-open eyes moved, watching each other. Then she took a step out of my lap. I put my hands around her. Flaring orange, Spot climbed down his branch and came to a stop at the cage entry. Standing tall, he bobbed his head again and again. She slipped out of my hands. Dropping her back, she went up into Spot's cage and flicked his face with her tongue.

"It's as though they recognize each other," I said.

"It doesn't always happen like that. Sometimes they fight."

The female lizard climbed up Spot's branch and settled herself under the basking lights. Spot followed and bobbed his big swollen head up and down, again and again.

"What will you name her?"

"I don't know. What do you think?"

"Well, what about Fern, since she's so green and pretty."

"She needs a more elegant name. She looks like a queen, stretched out along that branch. How about Cleopatra?"

"No, because then you'll start calling her Cleo and that's a clown's name. What about Jane, like in Tarzan?"

I thought of Tarzan's Jane, up in the trees, running in the jungle, climbing on vines. "Yeah, I like it."

"So how was your day?" Walter said.

"Not great." I reached over and shut the cage door. "There are these boys at school who make fun of me."

"You're kidding. What the heck for?"

I picked at my shoelaces. "I can't talk about it."

After a moment Walter said, "Oh, oh—that. They're just immature."

"That's what Nick says."

"Who's Nick?"

"This guy at school my friend Cathy is trying to get me to like."

"And?"

"What?"

"Do you?"

"I don't know. He's okay." Nick didn't really do anything or say anything that wasn't nice. He just made me uncomfortable. "He's one of those athletic types," I said.

Walter leaned his chin on his knees. "I was going to ask if you wanted to go to the zoo."

"Well, yeah, of course! When?"

"Saturday?"

"Isn't it hard to get there?"

"No, it's okay—I go all the time."

Saturday morning Walter and I stood on the subway platform and waited for the train to the Bronx. Walter was looking at Badmouth on my jacket.

"I wish I was good at painting, like you," he said. "If I could do that I'd paint herps all over my clothes."

"I bet you could if you tried."

"No, I flunked art."

"Einstein flunked math. Maybe you're like him with art."

"I doubt it," he said.

A stale wind blew out of the tunnel and then we saw head-lights coming. The train arrived and we found seats together.

As we traveled uptown, passengers kept getting off, and by the time the train went above ground we had the car nearly to ourselves. Bright light made us squint while our eyes adjusted. The buildings were lower and older than the towering office buildings downtown. Each time the doors opened at a stop, freezing cold air swirled around our legs. We shivered and pushed our hands down inside our pockets.

Walter pulled the backpack he'd brought onto his lap and unzipped it partway. "I fixed us lunch."

Inside the backpack were two water bottles, two oranges, and two sandwiches on whole-grain bread. "You're into healthy food," I said.

He reached in deeper and pulled out a bag of cookies. "Chocolate chip with pecans. I made them last night." Walter opened the bag and offered it to me. I took one.

"Oh, they're really good."

He smiled and zipped up the backpack.

The zoo seemed deserted. "All the people are inside the buildings," Walter said.

We walked past huge, bare sycamore trees and frozen ponds, and past the primate house and the big cats. The sky was a cold, clear blue, and the pale sun was flat and far away.

Walter was right about the people being inside the buildings. The reptile house was crowded. Voices filled halls lit only by the lights inside the displays.

"Don't worry," he said, leading me through the crowd. "We'll be seeing the animals from the other side."

He found the outline of a door in the wall and knocked. After a minute the door opened and a man wearing a white shirt and dark trousers looked out.

"Hey, Walter!" said the man, shaking Walter's hand. "Come in, come in."

"Mike, this is my friend Grace. She's been helping us around the shop."

Mike put out his hand and we shook. "Hi, Grace."

I liked him right away.

"I've got a meeting," Mike said. "But after that I'll show you the chameleons. How's Pops?"

"Doing fine, Mike, thanks." Walter said to me, "Mike helped Pops get the shop going years ago."

"That's right, back when Walter was just a tadpole."

"Mike thinks he's funny."

"Why don't you kids put your things in my office."

We followed Mike down a hall to a room with a desk and a couple of chairs. Books and stacks of papers covered every surface. Bony white tortoise shells and skeletons of giant frogs and of a lizard with wings lined the top of a bookshelf.

I took off my jacket and sweatshirt and hung them over the back of a chair.

"That's quite a marvelous jacket, Grace," Mike said. "Did you do the work?"

"Yes, she did," Walter said. "That's the iguana we had at the shop, Mike, remember?"

"Sure I do."

"He lives with me now," I said proudly.

"Well," Mike said, "Grace needs the shirt, don't you think?"

"Absolutely," Walter said.

Mike went to the closet and dragged out a cardboard box. He pulled out a gray T-shirt and held it up to show me. Across the front it said BRONX ZOO REPTILE HOUSE, spelled out in little snakes and lizards, just like on the shirt Walter had.

"Oh, it's so wonderful," I said, taking the shirt. My throat felt thick, but I managed to say thank you. I held the T-shirt in my hands a moment and then folded it neatly and tucked it inside my backpack.

Mike looked at his watch. "Walter, give Grace the tour and I'll find you when the meeting's over."

"Come on," Walter said. "There's a lot to see."

We went down a narrow hall with offices on one side and pairs of panels in the wall on the other. The panels had little windows in them, right at eye level. Through one panel we could look in and see the displays. The other panel looked into shift cages, where the snakes and lizards were held while the displays were being cleaned.

Walter stopped in front of a panel. "This one is really cool. The cobras always know when someone's back here."

It was true—we looked in at the Egyptian cobra and he was uncoiling himself and moving toward us fast. He rose up and looked right at us, with his shiny round dark eyes and his tongue flicking in and out. I put my fingers up to the narrow screened opening and the cobra flicked them with his tongue. I couldn't believe I was so close.

"What are those for?" I pointed to eye goggles hanging from a hook on the wall behind us. The lenses had splotches of white stuff on them, like dried salt.

"Goggles for the spitters. The white stuff is dried venom. Their aim is excellent."

Walter showed me all kinds of vipers—Russel's, Gaboon, rhinoceros—with intricate patterned skin that looked as though it would feel like velvet. Other vipers, like the saw-scaled and the puff adder, had skin that looked rough. We saw Gila monsters with their black-and-orange-beaded skin in their desert habitat, and tiny poison arrow frogs, colored red, yellow, blue, and black, hopping around the mossy floor of their terrarium. Spidery bromeliads and orchids grew from branches above, their leaves and tendrils hanging down, making a green paradise behind glass.

Down another hall was an enormous Nile monitor, in a glass enclosure that was larger than my bedroom.

"He's gotta be eight feet and over a hundred pounds," Walter said.

Speckled black and white all over, with the same restless eyes, the monitor was a giant version of the one who'd been at Fang & Claw. I could have stood still for hours, admiring his perfect lizardness.

"I'm getting hungry," Walter said.

We went back to Mike's office and pulled chairs up to his desk. Walter pushed aside a stack of New York Herpetological Society journals and put out the sandwiches he had made.

"Thank you for bringing me," I said.

"Mmm." Walter swallowed a bite of sandwich. "We can come back anytime."

"That was so great of Mike to give me the shirt. I feel like I got initiated into a club, or something."

"Yeah, it was a design that didn't go over big in the gift shop. So the reptile house staffers took them, and now it's the cool thing to have one." He took a drink from his water bottle and twisted the cap back on. "Anyway, there's more to see."

I gathered up the plastic wrap and orange peels and dropped them in the trash. Walter put the bag of cookies away in his backpack.

"Let's go have a look upstairs."

Big round and oval galvanized troughs, same as the ones used for horses, crowded the upper area, which was like a huge attic. Basking lights suspended from rafters hung over the troughs, some of which were covered with screened frames. In the troughs were snakes, tortoises, water turtles, young caimans, and alligators.

Walter leaned on the edge of a trough with a fat diamondback rattler stretched out on a wide piece of slate that was heated from below.

"There's usually a cool story that goes along with the animals up here," Walter said. "Like one time, the cops got a call about a bad smell coming from the top floor of an apartment building. When no one answered they broke in and found this guy in bed—he'd been dead a few days—and they found more than a hundred snakes, all of them poisonous. Some real beauties, like Amazonian corals and spectacled cobras and eyelash vipers."

"Did he get bitten?"

"No, it was a heart attack. You'd be surprised how many calls the police get about big snakes turning up in boiler rooms where they'd been living off rats. I think they ought to leave the snakes alone and quit using rat poison. And we ought to stop spraying for roaches and turn the Tokay geckos loose."

"A romantic notion, Walter." Mike came up behind us. "Come see the chameleons."

He led us to a room and unlocked the door. The room was lit up with pale violet light from full-spectrum bulbs, like in Walter's apartment, and the air was slightly cooler and wetter, the way it is during a spring rain. Mike opened a tall cage that was so filled with plants and leafy vines it was as though someone had cut a block out of the rain forest. He reached inside and carefully lifted out a chameleon. "Here she is. One of fifteen of our first captive-born Mount Meru Jackson's chameleons."

Her eyes moved independently, taking everything in.

When Mike set the chameleon on Walter's hand she wrapped her tail around his thumb and held on to his finger with mittenlike hands and feet. Walter looked like a little kid in a state of wonder. The chameleon's movements were slow, deliberate, like some great Tai Chi master. I thought she must have come from another world or another time.

Mike explained to us that her species was in trouble, because of deforestation. "But there's hope," he said. "The captive breeding program is going well." He smiled at the chameleon in Walter's hand. "These lizards are sensitive. If she starts turning gray and blotchy, we'll have to put her back."

Slowly, Walter held the chameleon out to me. She loosened her tail grip on his thumb and reached for me. When she grasped the tip of my finger with her delicate hand, I felt a shiver of delight. Rewrapping her tail around Walter's finger she came forward and took hold of mine with both hands. She watched me with one eye and rotated the other back to see Walter. I waited for her to walk all the way onto my hand, but her feet and tail stayed anchored on Walter. When his hand touched mine her skin began to turn the green of a new leaf. Walter and I smiled at each other.

After we put her back, we said goodbye to Mike and left the zoo. Walking to the subway station, I noticed a man up ahead, sitting in a truck, watching us.

"Hurry up," I said, taking Walter's arm.

The man made the squeaky kissing noise. Even in the cold my face burned.

When he did it again, Walter turned to look. "You know that guy? I think he's trying to get your attention."

"No kidding, Walter." I let go of his arm and hurried into the subway station.

"What?" Walter said, catching up.

"Look, he's just a creep, okay?"

"Oh. Sorry."

I sighed. I felt tired and defeated. "It's not your fault. I didn't mean to snap."

But I was still angry, and I was frustrated that Walter didn't understand. What was I supposed to do, explain it?

I sat on the train feeling humiliated and disgusting in this body that stuck out everywhere. I wished I were a lizard, all clean with scales and no hair or sweat or breasts or blood—none of that. I'd be sleek and graceful, not bulky and clumsy. I'd be powerful, with sharp teeth hidden behind flat, scaly lips, not these red, fleshy things I had. And I'd have eyes that could change—they could be dark and frightening, or they could be calm and unreadable.

Walter's eyes were shut, but I didn't think he was sleeping.

"Do you ever wish you were a lizard?" I asked. "Or a snake?"

He didn't answer right away. Then he opened his eyes. "No. Because then I wouldn't be able to enjoy looking at them and touching and holding them. And I wouldn't get to feel the way I do when I'm holding Badmouth."

"Well, I do. I wish I could turn into a Nile monitor."

"There's a tough lizard. Why do you wish that? Are you so unhappy as a person?"

"I hate the way I look."

"Grace, that's silly. I don't like the way I look, but getting upset about it doesn't help, believe me."

I kept quiet. I didn't see that he had a problem the way I did—he wasn't disgusting, like me. I felt him looking at me. I looked back at him, feeling cross.

"Do you want a cookie?" he asked. His eyes were calm and gray. They made me think of a spring morning in Mooresville, when the air was warm and still and a soft, steady rain fell.

"I would really like a cookie," I said.

—

Later I painted a Nile monitor on the other sleeve of my jacket. I made his claws sharp and his head rearing back in a hiss. I filled the sleeve, making his black-and-white-speckled body as big as I could. I put curves in his tail all the way from the elbow to the wrist. His arms reached around to hold on to my shoulder, and his gold eyes glared out at the world, blazing with the glittering paint I had used.

Python ate everything. She was on rats already and I had moved her into the wooden case that Walter brought over. About every ten days her eyes turned milky blue, and a few days after that she shed her skin. It came off in hundreds of pieces and lay around her like snowflakes that did not melt. The patches of scaled skin were beginning to meet, stretching and pulling the zigzag pattern over her back and ribs to cover the naked places, so they were no longer like wounds but instead like the pale pink skin underneath a healing scab. Her body had grown thick as my wrist. Sometimes she sat coiled outside of her hide box, with one orange eye looking out. Maybe she watched for rats. I knew when she slept, because her head leaned to one side, limp and settled against her body, her eye still, her ribs moving in and out steady and slow. When my footsteps woke her she leveled her head and her eyes moved. Her breath quickened and her tongue flicked in and out.

Cathy and I sat at our table in the coffee shop. Her puffy down coat lay over the back of her chair and she looked soft all over, with her wavy blond hair and flushed cheeks and green velvet dress. The dress had a long, flowing skirt and long sleeves, and the velvet clung to her body and showed her shape. I wondered how she did it—how she went around looking like such a girl and feeling good about it. Of course, her body was slender and the curves were a lot smaller than mine.

"I like your dress," I said.

"Thanks. They're on sale over in the Village. Let's get you one. They have other colors."

"That's okay. It wouldn't look good on me."

"Oh, please. When are you going to give it up?"

"Well, it's true. If they call me Chester now, what do you think they would say if I showed up in a curvy deal like that?"

"Who cares? They'll be speechless!"

"Thanks, I'll stick to my jacket and jeans."

Cathy clicked her coffee cup with a fingernail. "The jacket is really cool. But you know what? Time to outgrow it. I don't even know how you stay warm when it's freezing out."

"The sweatshirt is thermal-lined and I've got a sweater underneath."

"That's so ridiculous. You think you're hiding your figure, but you're not. In fact, you look bigger with all that on."

That made me mad and I kept quiet, because she was right. I felt awkward and stuffed. "So how come none of the boys at school bother you?" I asked finally.

"I don't let them."

"What, you threaten to beat them up, so now they're scared of you?"

"No, silly. I don't let their little act get to me."

"It's not just the boys at school. There's always some jerk on the subway looking at me funny and guys on the street making noises at me."

Cathy frowned. "Why do you let that bug you?"

"It's only embarrassing and humiliating—no big deal, right?"

"Don't get upset, Grace. Ignore it if you don't like it. You're not going to make it stop, you know. Act like you don't care. Really, why don't you take it as a compliment?"

"Because it's *not* a compliment. It's disgusting. They're not saying I'm pretty. I'm not stupid!"

Cathy smiled at me. "I never said you were stupid. Paranoid, maybe."

I wanted to be mad at her, but she started tickling my leg with the toe of her boot, and then I smiled too. I couldn't help it.

One day I climbed up my ladder and saw Spot pressed against Jane, biting her neck. He had a big piece of her skin in his teeth. I opened the cage to get him off her, but then I stopped. Spot was rubbing on her the way he had rubbed on my leg. Jane raised her tail to one side, and the sex part of Spot—purple-red, as thick as my little finger—came out from underneath his tail. He pushed himself between the pale green folds under Jane's tail, and then he bit down harder and they moved and struggled together. After a while Spot let go of Jane and licked her blood from his lips. She sat there as though everything was fine. I shut the cage door and went back down the ladder.

—

"Walter!" I said, rushing into Fang & Claw. "Guess what?"

"Look," Walter said, pointing at the big case where Sue and Albert were. "They've been at it since last night."

I stood next to Walter and we watched the big snakes. They were pressed together, their bodies wrapped around each other, black and gold patterns blending and separating and twisting, smooth muscles pushing and gliding. When their heads passed behind the glass, I saw their noses nuzzling and tongues flicking, and then I saw their tails locked together near the ends. I thought about the eggs that would come and how Sue would wrap around them until they hatched.

"Spot and Jane, they're doing that, too," I told Walter.

"So they're a pair for sure."

"What about Jane's eggs?"

"When the time comes we'll make her a nest box. You should also think about a bigger cage. I can help with that if you want."

"That'd be great."

"We'd better get a few things done around here. I've gotta do that rock python, and maybe you want to get started on the smaller snakes?"

"Okay."

The "smaller" snakes included Pete the pine snake, and I loved feeding him. The part I didn't like was killing mice, but I'd learned to do it fast, like Walter. I went to the back room and did that, and then I was ready to start feeding. Walter had opened the rock python's case and was changing the water.

I went down the row with my forceps and my handful of mice, thinking about where a bigger cage would fit in my room. Maybe I could move my bed downstairs.

From the corner of my eye I saw a flash of movement and felt an impact. The rock python had my hand, making me drop the mice. As quickly as he'd struck, he let go and withdrew his black and gold head, shifting his jaws, realigning the teeth. I raised my hand and turned it slowly and stared at the bite. It looked like it ought to hurt, but I didn't feel anything except warm blood and saliva running down my arm.

"Grace!" Walter cried, dropping the water bowl. He took my wrist and led me to the sink.

"Oh, my," Pops said, opening the first-aid box.

Walter held my hand under cold water. Then it hurt. A purple patch was growing under the skin, under the ellipse of puncture wounds.

"Now it hurts," I said, keeping calm.

"I bet. He punctured a vessel." Walter squeezed my wrist to make the blood flow. I rolled my eyes.

Pops twisted the lid off a bottle of peroxide.

"Here, Dad. Give it to me."

Walter poured peroxide over my hand, and the pink bubbly stuff dripped into the sink. The door opened up front. "Anybody home?" called a voice.

"Mice are on the floor out there," I said. "And the python's case is open."

Pops went up front to take care of things and tend the customer.

"It didn't hurt before," I said to Walter. "I barely felt his teeth."

Still holding my wrist, Walter dug around in the box and found some packages of gauze. He ripped two open with his teeth and put the square patches on the bite. "Hold it there," he said, and I did while he wrapped tape over the gauze.

Walter smoothed the bandage, pressing gently here and there. His hands felt warm and nice and he stopped smoothing the bandage for a moment and looked at me. Then he lifted my hand and tried to make it better with a kiss. I jerked it away, which made the bite sting.

"I'll do it," I said, covering my wounded hand with the other.

"Sorry," Walter said. His face was red. He turned away.

I turned off the faucet and heard Pops ask, "How's the patient?"

"She's fine," Walter said.

Then it was quiet except for the crickets chirping. "Walter," I said, "thanks for taking care of my hand."

"Oh, sure." He didn't look up. "It shouldn't get infected, I don't think."

Pops said, "You look wobbly. I'll get some aspirin from my office."

I fumbled around, mopping up spilled water from the rock python's bowl while I held up my hand to keep it from throbbing. Walter busied himself cleaning the glass on the case.

"Where'd Pops get to with that aspirin?" Walter said, breaking the silence. He sounded mad.

The gate opened, and a black hairy muzzle appeared in the doorway. It was Nitely, with Cathy and Nick. I could feel many of the animals in the shop recoiling. A few of them perked up with interest.

"Cathy, he can't come in here," I said.

"Who, Nitely or Nick?" She laughed. "I'll tie him up outside."

"Sorry," I whispered to Walter. "I don't know what they're doing here."

"It's okay. They're welcome to look around."

Cathy walked in. She was wearing another of her flowing dresses. Nick followed her.

"Hi, Walter." Then Cathy looked at my hand. "Hey, what happened to you?"

"Just a little bite. I got careless."

Nick came closer. "Does it hurt?"

"No!"

Nick shrugged. He took off his jacket, slung it over his shoulder, and looked around. "Whoa, this place is for real."

"Cathy, how did you find me?" I was kind of annoyed that she had.

"Duh. I looked in the phone book. Hey, Walter," Cathy said, "this is Nick, a friend of ours from school."

Nick put out his hand and Walter shook it. The door opened again. A man came in, carrying a box with a handle on it.

"Hiya, Walt. Pops around?"

"Sure, in the office. Go on down."

The man went behind the curtain. Nick looked at Sue

and Albert. "Hey, a wrestling match," he said. "Check it out, Cath."

"Looks kind of sexy to me."

"Cathy!" I snapped.

"Yes," Walter said, "actually they're—"

"It's nothing!" I pushed between Nick and the glass, with my bandaged hand up in the air.

"You're acting weirder than usual," Cathy said.

Nick winked at me.

Cathy put her arm through mine. "Anyway, we're meeting Dan and going to the movies. Don't say you've got home-work—it's Friday."

"Excuse me," Walter said. "I've got animals to feed."

"Yeah, me too," I said.

Cathy held on to my arm. "But you're coming with us."

"I'm pretty busy here."

Then Walter said, "I can take care of things here if you want to go. You can't do much with that bandage on, anyway."

"Exactly," Cathy said.

I pulled my arm away from Cathy. "I don't feel like going to the movies."

Cathy sighed impatiently. "What can I tell you, Nick?"

He just shrugged.

After they left, Walter went to the back room to get crickets. I followed him.

"How come you wanted me to leave?"

"That guy likes you," he said.

"No."

"He does."

"How do you know?"

"He didn't come to see snakes. Here, since you're helping." He handed me the feeding jar to hold while he caught crickets.

"Why on earth would he like me?"

Walter dropped a second handful of crickets into the jar and put the lid back on the tank. "Because you're pretty." He put out his hand for the jar. "I'll take that."

I gave it back and followed him up front again. "I'm not, though. I'm *not* pretty. And you were trying to get rid of me and now you're acting … treating me funny."

Walter let his shoulders drop and gave out a heavy sigh. "I thought you wanted to go with your friends."

"I didn't. I wanted to be here." I found the mice and finished feeding snakes.

Walter opened the cabinet with the tarantulas and scorpions and started feeding them crickets. When he took down the white jar with the Brazilian spider inside, I came to watch. He lifted the lid and there was a soft ripping sound. Tattered threads of white silk floated out from the mouth of the jar and hung in the air. Walter tipped the jar so I could see inside. He took out his forceps and tore the silk. I jumped when fangs and legs hit the metal, fighting, making a clinking that I could feel. Walter pulled the forceps away. Four of the spider's black hairy legs framed the tear in the silk, waiting, two on each side of her curved fangs.

"I don't think she's ever going to accept a mate," he said.

—

On the subway home I was angry with Walter. I felt bad about pulling my hand away when all he was going to do was kiss it. But he had looked at me and I'd felt weird all of a sudden and it was like a reflex. I read the ads on the wall. They were all about bodies and making them perfect. Miracle diets, permanent hair removal, health clubs, exercise classes. There was laser treatment for varicose veins and scars from acne. And there was cosmetic surgery. "Breast augmentation," they called it. There were even "before" and "after" pictures. I squirmed in my seat and looked away.

My eyes wandered back to the cosmetic surgery ad. And I sat up straight and wondered why I hadn't noticed before. The last procedure on the list was "breast reduction."

"Mom," I said, throwing my backpack on a chair as soon as I got home.

"Well, hi yourself." She sat reading a huge textbook that lay open on the table.

"I want to have breast-reduction surgery."

She looked up at me and smiled. "I know, honey. Being a teenager is a real drag sometimes." Then she saw the bandage. She took off her glasses. "What happened to your hand?"

"It's fine, just a little bite. Listen, I'm serious. I saw an ad on the subway and I'm going to get a real job to pay for it."

"Grace, that's absurd. And I'm sorry you feel that way, because you have a lovely figure."

"I don't! I hate it! All I ever get are boys making fun of me at school and men on the street going *pssst* and making sick, disgusting noises at me. I hate it, Mom!" I glared at her and folded my arms across my chest, bumping the bandage and making the bite sting.

"Oh, honey. You *will* grow into your body; you've just got to be patient with yourself."

"It's easy for you to say that—you have small breasts."

That got rid of her smile. "I'd gladly trade figures with you, Grace, if it were at all possible."

"But it *is* possible—I can have them removed!"

"When you're eighteen you can do whatever you want. But I hope you learn to like yourself the way you are, long before that."

Later, when my mother went out, I sat in her chair and flipped through the immense art book she'd been studying. It was filled with paintings of nude figures and I slammed it shut. Freda made one of her flirty sounds and jumped into my lap. She moved around, trying to get comfortable. She wanted me to pet her, but I didn't; I pushed her off me and went to my room. I wanted to paint some snakes on my jeans.

The next day Cathy found me in the library.

"I knew you'd be here," she said, pulling up a chair. "I'm having a party to finish off the spring break. I'm telling you now because you keep wriggling out of things. This time, you're coming."

"Won't you make brownies, like you used to?"

"Brownies are fattening. But okay, I'll make some. How's the hand?"

"It's fine."

"Uh-huh." She crossed her legs and adjusted the fabric of her skirt. "Don't you think you're kind of getting carried away with the lizard-snake thing?"

"I already said it was an accident—I was being careless with food animals."

"It's not just that. Look, the jacket is one thing, but now you've got snakes on your jeans. It's too much."

"What do you mean?"

"Grace, you've painted snakes coming up your thighs. Please don't be so naïve."

"I don't know what you're talking about." But as I said it, I did know. She was right, and I felt stupid for not seeing before. And it made me angry that that was the way things were.

Cathy saw how I felt, and her expression changed. "Poor baby," she said. "Why is all this so hard for you? I can't understand why you're so mortified by becoming a woman."

"It's disgusting."

"Okay, adolescence is a little messy sometimes. So? You can't *not* go through it."

"I don't have to like it."

"Yes, but you're miserable so much of the time."

"What am I supposed to do, celebrate?"

"Why not? Stop fighting it. Embrace the inevitable."

"You're worse than my mom! Look at you and your slim body—you don't have to deal with enormous, gross things like I've got!"

Cathy narrowed her eyes at me. "Stop!" She took my face in her hands and gave me a noisy kiss on the cheek. "You *will* come to my party," she said. Then she stood up and walked out of the library.

I went into the girls' bathroom and stood in front of the mirror. I had swelled up even bigger, the way I always did for part of every month. My head ached and I had zits and I was sweaty and my hair was stringy and the longer I looked at myself the more I hated me. And Cathy said I should "embrace" it.

The bathroom door opened and Helen walked in, wearing a cute lavender top that clung to her small, unmoving breasts. She said hi and smiled at me like I was some poor, deformed alien. Tossing her shiny gold hair over her shoulder, Helen took out her lip-gloss, twisted the container open, and started putting the stuff on. It smelled like grape jelly.

When classes were over I shoved my books in my backpack and started down the stairs. It was noisy with footsteps and voices, but I heard, "*Chest*-er, *Chest*-er!" echoing down the stairwell. Two girls coming up the stairs looked at me, and I could tell they knew I was the one being made fun of. I glared at them like, *What are you looking at?* And then I remembered the time I got punched in the face at my old school for looking at another girl. Now I was becoming like that girl, mean and angry all the time.

On the subway I could see my angry face in the dark window. I tried to soften the lines by letting go of my creased forehead and rigid chin, but I couldn't do it.

More people got on as the train moved into Manhattan. I stood and took hold of the pole near the doors so I could get out when I needed to. At the next stop a man in a suit got on and held on to the pole. He stood facing me, and pretty soon I could feel him looking at me. My skin prickled. I turned and squeezed through the crowded car to get away, and then I realized that the train was pulling into Fourteenth Street. I couldn't get out in time. I stood rigid with anger as the doors rattled shut on my Fang & Claw stop. I had to close my eyes for a second to keep from bursting and striking out against all the bodies pressing against me. When the train stopped at Twenty-third Street, I pushed my way out and ran up the stairs out of the station.

I had nine blocks to walk to Fang & Claw. Even though it was raw and drizzling, I was hot. I unzipped my sweatshirt and pushed the damp hair off my forehead. My breath came out steaming, like a dragon's, and my jaw ached from clenching my teeth. I didn't want to bring any of this into Fang & Claw so I took a deep breath and slowed down. Just five blocks to go, and everything would be okay when I got there. I walked, breathing in and out, and watched the sidewalk go by under my feet.

Sensing someone approach, I looked up as a boy hardly older than me swerved in close. He said, "Snaky-girl!" in a whispery voice and flicked out his tongue by my ear and kept going.

I pressed my hands against my ears and nearly stumbled—it had happened so fast—and he was gone before I could react. I didn't want to turn and look behind me, so I kept walking. My legs were heavy and numb.

Outside Fang & Claw I stood still for a second. My face

wasn't burning anymore; now it felt cold. And I felt as though I might just break. Forcing myself to smile, I pushed the gate aside and went in. Pops was with a customer over by the colubrid snakes. Walter was cleaning out the turtle tanks.

"Grace, hi. You look pale. You all right?"

"I'm fine. It's cold out."

"Okay," he said, still looking at me.

"What needs doing?"

"The frogs—misting and feeding. When you get to the feeding, I'll give you a hand."

I hung up my jacket and sweatshirt and took the spray bottle and filled it. Then I got the cricket jar and held it in one hand while I gathered a few handfuls of the brown, leggy bugs with the other. If only I hadn't been so slow, I could have dealt with that boy. I could have caught him by the collar of his coat and—what? Bitten him? I was pathetic. My hand shook; I dropped the jar, and broken glass and crickets went everywhere. I gritted my teeth to keep from swearing. Walter came back, got down on his knees, and started catching crickets.

"I'm sorry," I said. "I'm such a clumsy idiot—I—my hand— it just slipped and I lost my grip—" I had to bite my lip to keep it from trembling.

"It's okay," Walter said. He stood to get the broom and dustpan. "It's happened to me before, too." He started to sweep up the broken glass.

"Let me do that. I'm the jerk who made this mess!"

Walter stopped and looked at me. "Are you sure you're okay?"

My shoulders slumped. I let the air out of my chest. "No one will leave me alone, and I'm supposed to ignore all the rude comments and looks and go on like everything's fine and normal. I mean, how can things be normal when I've got these huge *growths* on me? What's normal about that?"

Walter was blushing and I stopped.

"I'm sorry," I said. "I shouldn't talk about that stuff."

He shook his head. "It's okay. I'm sorry you feel that way about yourself."

"You sound like my mother! Can't just one person agree with me? Can't just one person say, 'Yeah, Grace—you're disgusting, all right.' Why does everyone have to keep telling me to accept myself the way I am, especially when *they* don't!" I glared at Walter. "You're never a mess, you're always right and good and calm and okay. Why do you get to be *okay* all the time? I mean, look at you, you're—you look like a frog!"

Walter looked at me. Water trickled from the faucet. My legs were cement; I couldn't breathe. Walter blinked. "Actually, I'm not okay all the time. But I try not to be mean to my friends."

Walter's face was stone and his cheeks were red. He put down the broom and dustpan. I caught his arm. "Walter, I'm sorry."

He pulled his arm away gently, turned, and went to finish cleaning the turtle tanks. I was as cold and stiff as a snake in the snow, but I made myself pick up the broom and sweep up the glass. I emptied the dustpan into the trash. Then I put on my sweatshirt and jacket and left because I'd started to cry, and that was pathetic, to cry like a dumb girl in front of Walter.

I ran past the subway station and kept running, wiping my eyes and nose on my sleeve, going down side streets, avoiding people. I felt as though I was in a bad dream, being pulled farther and farther away from ever being happy again, but I was the one pulling and I couldn't stop. I ran all the way home to my room and went up the ladder, opened Spot's cage, and took him and pulled him to me and held on, rubbing my cheek against his rough, scaly shoulders. Soon my heart stopped pounding so hard.

"Spot," I said, "you're *here*."

As I hugged him and kissed him I realized that he had been here all along. Even though he had his mate now, he was still Spot, still right here, letting me hold on to him. Keeping one hand on his back, I reached for Jane and petted her and told her with my eyes that I loved her, too.

When my mother came home she looked at me and said, "What happened, Grace?"

I told her how my day at school went and about being on the subway and how I dropped the cricket jar. "I was so angry and I couldn't hold it in anymore, Mom. I said something horrible to Walter."

"Okay, but surely you can apologize."

"I did. I said I was sorry, but he walked away from me."

"Maybe he needs time. Maybe you do too. Try and be patient with things, Grace. Take tomorrow off. Stay home and be with your lizards."

I said okay. New tears came—relief tears, mixing with sad ones.

In the morning I had coffee with my mother. I fixed us toast and eggs, and she gave me a hug and went to her classes. I washed the dishes and then sat back down at the table with another cup of coffee. My eyes welled up when I thought about Walter. What came over me to make me be so horrible? A tiny something pricked at me—something to do with the disturbing way he looked at me as he tried to kiss my hand. I couldn't figure it out. But what I said was wrong. Walter could never deserve that, no matter what.

I didn't feel like doing anything. I just sat there. I looked at the clock. Everyone was in math class by now.

At noon I pictured Cathy in the cafeteria, sipping coffee, laughing with her other friends. I imagined the way she tore open the blue packets of fake sugar and shook them into her coffee, and how her earrings dangled when she laughed. I thought about the smiles she gave me when I gave her only sour looks and how she was always pushing me to have some fun in spite of everything. I tipped my cup and looked at the dark, thick stuff at the bottom, and then I drank it and chewed the grounds.

I went up to my bed and opened the cage door so Spot and Jane could come out if they wanted. Then I lay down and started to read. But I kept reading the same paragraph over and over. I put the book down and looked at the ceiling, at the dingy, peeling paint. Walter's room wasn't like that; it was bright with clean, smooth walls.

It occurred to me that I had never really moved in. For all that time I'd been waiting, thinking that any day my mother would snap out of it and we'd go home to Mooresville. It wasn't true; it wasn't going to happen.

Spot had climbed out of the cage and was stretched out at my feet. Jane was sitting close to the edge of the platform—too close. I sat up and pulled her onto my lap. It made me think that having a bigger cage up in the loft was a bad idea. I peeled loose skin off Jane's toes and thought about it for a minute. Why couldn't I turn the whole space under my loft into a lizard room? I wanted a place I could go into, where I could be with the lizards, instead of always being on the outside, looking in at them. I wanted a place where all three of us could be happy and comfortable together.

I settled Jane beside Spot, opened my sketchbook and started to make a drawing of the room. It seemed like all I had to do was put up one wall with a door in it and then arrange branches and lights and plants inside.

My mother built stretchers for her paintings, and I was sure that she could help me build my room. When she came home I showed her the drawing. "I want to put some fresh paint in my loft, too."

She put on her glasses and looked at the drawing. Then she took a tape measure into my room. I followed to see what I could do. I watched her pull out the tape and measure from the floor to the underside of the loft platform.

"Next week is spring break," I said, hopeful. She was so busy, always working or studying. "Can I do it then? I think I need help making the wall."

She took a pen from my desk and wrote numbers on the

drawing. "We can do this in a day. Starting in the morning, first thing."

"What about classes?"

"We're cutting. Now, we need a list."

We sat down at the kitchen table. I kept my hands in my lap and tried not to scratch the scabby skin where the rock python had bitten me. Freda jumped up in Mom's lap, but she didn't let that interrupt.

"They'll have a door in stock at the hardware place on Canal. Instead of sheetrock we'll use pine boards—that'll be nice and so much easier. We'll need to rent a cut-off saw and a screw gun. And we need fasteners, a couple of hinges, a doorknob, angle brackets. That's it. Oh—the paint: you'll pick a color. You should scrape that ceiling first and prime it. So you need a drop cloth, a roller and sleeve, and a brush."

She put down the pen and we looked at each other.

"This'll be good," she said.

My mother woke me at sunrise with a cup of coffee. She was dressed in paint-smeared jeans and sneakers and an old sweat-shirt. "Hardware store opens at eight."

It took three trips to get all the stuff back to our place. We lugged boards and cans of paint up the stairs.

"You and the lizards won't want to sleep in here for a night," Mom said. "Then the fumes will clear."

She helped me pull my bed down and set it up next to hers, and while she put on the sheets I fixed a place for Spot and Jane on the couch. I twisted a heat bulb into the reading lamp socket and the lizards stretched out along the back of the couch, underneath the light. Then we moved Python's case out and set it with the window facing away from the lizards.

I went up the ladder and took down the dinosaur and reptile posters and the picture of the swamp on the ceiling and rolled them up and put them away. Then I spread the drop cloth and went to work scraping the old paint off the ceiling. Paint chips kept falling in my eyes and my arms got sore and I had to keep switching the scraper from one hand to the other. Downstairs, my mom ran the saw, cutting boards for the wall.

Only once did I stop working—I went down and put Freda's food bowl up on the counter so Spot wouldn't eat it. I'd heard his claws clicking around on the floor and the clink of the cat's bowl and I knew what he was up to.

By noon all the boards were cut and I had a coat of primer on that was nearly dry. I started putting on paint while my mother nailed up boards.

Late that afternoon, when the wall was almost done, I helped my mom hang the door. Then she came up the ladder and took over with the paint roller while I cut in with the brush.

"Grace, I was wondering. What about Python? When will we build her a new cage?"

"She can be in the other part of my room."

"Okay. I'm curious, though. How big will she get?"

"Well, Badmouth is sixteen feet."

"Wow. Is it fair to keep her without a mate?"

I scratched an itchy spot of paint that was drying on my cheek. "No, it's not."

My mom didn't say anything more about Python. I knew she wouldn't make me give her up. She wanted me to think about it, though. But I was scared—what if someone else had her and didn't take care of her and she got sick again? The only person I could ever give her to was Walter.

I brushed paint into the last corner.

"Good timing," Mom said. "I need to get in there with the roller. Why don't you wash the brush and put the lid on the paint can. The tools go back in the hall closet."

I cleaned the brush and put away the tools, and then I got a box and filled it with the wood scraps. By the time I'd swept up the sawdust, Mom was finished painting.

It was the first of April and it wasn't dark out yet, and with new white paint on the walls, my room seemed to glow in the fading light. My mother and I stood for a moment in our paint-spotted clothes and looked at our work. She untied her scarf and let her hair fall down her back.

I opened the door to the lizard room and we went inside.

"When will you move them in?"

"First thing tomorrow. After I set up their branches and basking lights." I thought maybe I could put some hooks in the ceiling and hang plants, like in Walter's room.

My mother picked up a couple of screws from the window-sill. "Let's order a pizza."

After dinner, we got into bed, too tired to watch a movie. I kept turning and rearranging the covers. I got up for a drink of water and came back to bed. My mother rolled over on her side, facing me.

"Can't sleep?"

"I don't know what to do about Walter."

"Tell him exactly how you feel. Trust his friendship."

"It's hard, though."

"What is? Apologizing?"

"Talking about why I got angry and said what I said. It's embarrassing. I want it all to go away, but I know it won't."

I looked over at where the lizards were sleeping nose to nose. In the light from the street I could see the spiky outline of their crests, running the length of the couch like a long sea serpent.

"Guess I'll go to Fang & Claw tomorrow and see if Walter's around."

"Good plan."

I lay still and thought about the time when we left that dirty apartment in Colorado and drove all the way back to Mooresville. We stayed in a motel one night and she told me jokes until we fell asleep. Then while it was still dark we got up and ate waffles for breakfast at a diner. I remembered the smell of her coffee in the car and watching the sky ahead of us turning pink and orange and then bright yellow. I remembered how it felt to be in the car, just the two of us, going home.

I felt my mother reach for my hand. I took hold of hers and squeezed it. She squeezed back twice. I squeezed three times.

In the morning I started setting up lights, running the cords under the loft so the lizards couldn't pull on them. Mom helped me bring the cage down and take off its door. Standing on its end, the cage was a perfect piece of furniture. The lizards could climb up the screened sides and bask on top, right under the lights, and they could see out the window, too.

My mom left to work brunch at her waitress job. I was about to move Spot and Jane into their room when I heard toenails clicking and a leash jingling in the hall. I opened the door, and Nitely bolted in, pulling Cathy behind. The lizards dove off the couch and went scrambling around the edges of the room while Freda stood with her back arched, hissing.

"Nitely!" Cathy yelled, jerking on the leash. "Sorry, I didn't know they were out. I'll tie him up in the hall."

"No, it's okay, take him in my room. The lizards will get over it."

"Are you sure? Where's the snake?"

"Over there." I nodded at Python's case.

Cathy took Nitely into my room while I gathered up the stiff, wide-eyed bodies of Spot and Jane and put them back on the couch. They pressed themselves down between the cushions to hide.

"Relax," I told them. "You too, Freda."

Cathy had gone inside the new room. "It looks great in here. Is this what you've been doing the last few days?"

"Yeah, it's a room for the lizards. My mom stayed home from school to help."

"I thought you were sick."

"I was, kind of."

"You didn't miss much. Everyone was too wound up for spring break. So what are you doing? I'm meeting Dan at the park. Want to come along?"

"No. I've got to finish up here and move them in."

"What're you doing later?"

"Going to Fang & Claw."

"I thought that place was closed weekends."

"It is, but I need to try and find Walter."

"Uh-oh, I knew you two were in love!"

I shook my head.

"What?"

"I said something mean to him and I need to say sorry."

"What did you say?"

"I told him he looked like a frog."

Cathy covered her mouth to hide the smile. "I'm sorry, but—"

"Don't."

"Okay, go on. What did Prince Charming do to deserve it?"

"He didn't *do* anything. Not really. I got mad because he was telling me to accept myself the way I am, the same way my mother does. The same way you do."

"Well, you should."

I felt myself heating up. "Stop trying to fix me. Stop trying to make me be happy, because I can't be, not right now. I just have to get through it."

"It's hard to see you so unhappy, though."

"I haven't been very nice to my friends, huh? That's the unacceptable part."

"But there are ways to make up for that! Starting with coming to my party next Saturday, in case you forgot."

She untied Nitely's leash from the ladder. "Okay, you can bring Walter."

Later, when I made it to Fang & Claw, someone was there and the nerves in my stomach went wild.

But it was Pops who said, "Hello?" when I pushed open the gate, and I could tell that he was alone.

"Where's Walter?"

"He has gone to visit his mother for spring break. She lives in California."

"Why didn't he call me to help while he was away?"

Pops smiled. "He seemed to think you needed some time off. But I would be delighted to have your help and your company."

I smiled back, a little anxious because of how I'd treated Walter. I hung my jacket on its hook. "Shall I start with the turtles, then?"

"That would be great," Pops said. He went back to feeding the baby snakes.

We worked without talking much, only a question or comment about one of the animals passing between us now and then. I kept feeling little waves of shame. I felt like I should talk to Pops and explain why I hadn't come around the last few days. I had to say something.

"Pops?"

"Yes?"

"I was mean to Walter, that time I left in a hurry? I got angry and it just came out and it's not true. And I'm feeling terrible and sorry."

"You've been having a rough time, eh?"

He put the baby corn snake he was holding in my hands. The snake's tongue flicked in and out as he wove his rust and tan patterned body between my fingers.

Pops sat down on the stepladder as though he was happy to have a break. "They call him a corn snake because he is found sometimes in barns and silos, feeding on mice." He rested his hands on his knees. "Think how many times the young snake has to shed his skin while he grows up. Each time he sheds, his skin is dull, his eyes are dull, and he can't see. But each time he struggles and pushes to come out of the old skin, he has grown some."

Pops raised his woolly eyebrows. "And you know what? He never stops shedding until he dies. He is always growing."

The baby corn snake had coiled in the palm of my hand with his head resting in the center. His tongue stopped flicking, but his pupils moved, keeping watch, and partway down his body his ribs moved with each breath.

"Walter is a patient boy," Pops said, standing up. "Everything will be okay."

I went to help Pops every day. One afternoon he called out as I came in. "Sue has laid her eggs."

He took my hand and led me to the case where Sue and Albert had been together through the winter. Albert was back in his own case, and Sue was in the corner of hers. She held her clutch of eggs in the center of her thick coils. I could see a few eggs at the top of the clutch. They were the kind of soft white color that is unmistakably egg, and they were huge. Just one would fill my hand.

"How many?"

"I think close to fifty."

Sue's head lay across the top of the clutch. Now and again, her body quaked to keep her eggs warm. I wanted to be right there when they hatched and see the baby snakes with their pushed-up noses and big eyes and little forked tongues flicking, all spilled around their mother's great body.

"Walter will be excited," I said.

"Yes," Pops agreed.

Leaving Fang & Claw one day, I heard that *pssst!* noise coming out the doorway of a bar. I rolled my eyes. I was angry, but I didn't show it, and I could feel it pass as I kept walking.

There was another thing I figured out. I'd started reading a science fiction novel I bought at a street sale. It was about two boys who go back in time to when dinosaurs lived. I took it with me on the subway to read. It was great. I could even read standing if the train was crowded—I could hold on to the pole with one hand and have the book in the other. If someone was looking at me, I didn't care.

Before going to Fang & Claw, I spent time with Spot and Jane, sitting with them in their new room. Freda followed me in one morning and jumped into my lap. I petted her and she purred and kneaded my leg and looked up at me, squinting. I looked into her yellowy-green eyes. "You're so pretty, Freda."

She wasn't a lizard, though. I ran my fingers through her

soft fur and felt her warmth on my legs, but I couldn't get that deep-down feeling that made me catch my breath, the way I did when I touched scales or looked into the eyes of a lizard. I wondered why. After all, Freda was a mammal and so was I. Like it or not, I would always be a mammal, far away from relatedness to lizards, and it made me sad.

Python had shed again, and this time it came off in two pieces except for the skin that stuck to her face and eyes. When I lifted the top of her case she came up fast, flicking her tongue. I waited for her to smell that I didn't have food before I reached in. Sliding my hand under her chest, I took her tail in my other hand and lifted her onto my shoulders. She reached outward and swayed, tongue flicking the air, while the tip of her tail curled to find the belt loop on my jeans. She had grown so big and heavy I wondered how long I would be able to lift her.

I found the tweezers and sat down in the chair by the window. Python had tried to get the old skin off—the rostral shield was worn from rubbing against the walls of the case. Her tongue quit flicking and she didn't pull away when I held her head and slid the edge of the tweezers between old skin and new at her lip. Her tail curled and uncurled and her eyes moved, but she didn't struggle, even though her lips were tender around the heat pits. I clamped down on the tweezers and lifted the skin to where I could get my fingers under it and grasp more of it so it wouldn't tear. I peeled back the old skin and one eye cap came away; then I pulled up and over the top of her head, scale by scale, to the other eye, until that cap was off too.

Holding up the translucent mask of Python's face, I turned

it in the light to see the opal sheen. I let go of her head and she settled on my arm. Her skin had grown so that the gold and black zigzag pattern twisted all down her back and sides. I traced the scars with my finger and remembered how raw the wounds had been. Each time she shed, the scars became tougher. Sunset colors and blue and green shimmered across the light-refracting scales of her strong body. I could feel her strength.

The parties I knew about were ones with crowds of people and loud music. I'd been to those parties with my mother and I'd wandered around with a can of soda in my hand, watching people talking or dancing. I thought Cathy's party would be like that, with lots of kids from school and music and maybe dancing. I'd get to stand around and talk to Cathy and eat the brownies she had promised to make.

When I got to Cathy's it was quiet except for Nitely's barking.

"Oh, hush, Nitely," Cathy said. Her eyes were sleepy, and she wore a soft pink shirt that looked like pajamas. "What, no Walter?"

"He's away."

"Too bad. Anyway, let's get ready." She took my sleeve and pulled me back to her room. "Lose the jacket."

Cathy's closet was crammed full of clothes, mostly hers, but some that Ellen had left behind when she went away to college. I hung my jacket on the bedpost and watched Cathy search through the closet. She pulled a lacy white blouse off a hanger and gave it to me. "Try that."

Then she started going through a pile of shoes, tossing sandals and clogs aside. "I don't have anything that will fit. You'll have to go barefoot. Anything's better than those sneakers."

I put on the blouse and sat down on the bed to take off my sneakers. Cathy leaned over the dresser top with her face close to the mirror, putting black mascara on her eyelashes. Then she picked up a long pin with a pearl on the end and started to separate the lashes that stuck together. I looked in the mirror at her green eyes.

"Take this." She put a brush in my hand. "Brush your hair."

I stood up next to Cathy and pulled the brush through my hair, trying to get it to not be so flat. The lacy shirt was dumb. It did make me look different, though—softer, maybe.

Cathy fussed over her hair. The doorbell rang. "Well, someone's here," she said, putting down the brush.

I got a little bit nervous, wondering if it was Nick at the door. He made me edgy. It was a weird mix of feelings that wore me out. I kept checking the buttons on the blouse. Cathy walked out ahead of me, still wearing the pajama top. She opened the door and a tall, dark-haired guy came in.

She threw her arms around him and then she took his hand and with a big, eager smile she said, "Grace, this is Dan."

"Hi, Dan. Great to meet you."

"Cathy told me about your lizards."

I smiled. Cathy must think it was kind of neat, the way she was always telling everyone. "It's true," I said. "I love them."

The bell rang again and a group of kids from the senior

class walked in. Helen was with them, looking like a Valentine in her red velvet top and matching lips. I put my hands in my pockets and followed Cathy to the sound system. Soon everyone was moving around the cooler, popping soda bottle tops, grabbing handfuls of pretzels, and sitting down in big, stuffed chairs and on the rug in the living area.

Cathy loaded CDs into the stereo, turned it on, and crossed the room to where Dan was sitting on the couch. She patted the cushion beside her. "Come sit, Grace."

I sat down. Nitely jumped up in my lap, pinning me to the couch.

Cathy laughed. "He's always been in love with Grace," she told Dan.

Then Nick came in.

"Nick!" Cathy yelled. "Sit with us! Nitely, get down."

"Oh, he can stay," I said.

Cathy took Nitely's collar and pulled him off my lap. Nick walked over and sat down next to me.

"Grace," he said, "good to see you."

"Hi, Nick."

Cathy and Dan were kissing, so I had to turn toward Nick. He was close enough that I could feel heat coming from him.

"Are you uncomfortable?" he asked.

"No, I'm—I've got a cramp in my foot." I started drawing circles in the air with my big toe, pretending to concentrate.

"I totally understand. Muscle cramps are the worst." He shook his head. "Where's your jacket? The one with the crawlies painted on?"

"In Cathy's room. What do you mean, 'crawlies'?"

He shrugged innocently. "Snakes, lizards. It looks good on you."

"Oh? You think so? Cathy's always trying to get me to wear dresses."

"Nah, you don't need that."

I folded my arms—he was trying to flatter me.

"It's like me, with wrestling?" he went on. "It's my thing and I need to wear it wherever I go. I think it's great to be passionate about something." He nodded his head up and down sincerely, as though agreeing with himself. I couldn't help but think of the way Spot bobbed his head.

"Yeah," I said.

I wished Walter were there. I didn't just wish it, I wanted it badly. I wanted to be sitting beside Walter and hearing about his visit to California, and I couldn't wait for him to see the new lizard room. I couldn't wait to give him Python.

"Excuse me," I said.

Nick nodded his head again and I nearly laughed. I went back to Cathy's room and sat down on her bed. Nitely followed. He jumped up and lay beside me and looked at me with his forehead scrunched over his glassy brown eyes. I scratched his ears.

"Good boy," I said.

He thumped the bed with his tail. I took off the lacy blouse and put on my old shirt and sneakers and jacket. I looked at myself in the mirror, with Spot on one sleeve and the Nile monitor on the other. Even though I'd wanted the monitor to be fierce and mean, he wasn't. I could see my love for him in the way I had painted him. That was why I painted the lizards on my jacket. Not to keep people away, but to always have lizards near.

I saw a place where one more lizard could go. The chameleon that Walter and I had held at the zoo would sit perfectly on the front, right over the pocket. When she was done I would give the jacket to Walter.

In the other room, everyone was sitting in a big circle on the rug, playing a game with cards and spoons in the middle. It looked like fun, with all the cards moving around the circle fast and then the shrieking and squealing when everyone grabbed for a spoon or tried to take one away from someone else. Then there was all that kissing going on while a new round of cards was dealt. I saw that Nick was sitting next to Helen. The absence of his attention felt funny for a second, but then it was a relief.

I made my way to the door, not wanting to interrupt the game. Halfway down the stairs, I heard Cathy. "Grace, wait."

I turned. She folded her arms and leaned against the doorframe.

"So here you go again, running off in the night. What are you after? Your lizard love?"

I smiled up at her. "I had a nice time. Call you tomorrow?"

"Call me tomorrow."

I hurried down the stairs, pushed open the street door, and stopped to breathe the spring night air. Few people were out and I had the sidewalks to myself. The nighttime city lights softened things. There was no glare of steel and glass, no sharp, hard lines or edges, no fast-moving traffic. The city felt calm yet wide awake, not waiting, not hurrying, just being. Like a lizard. It made me want to walk. I went by the pizza place Cathy and I used to go to, past the park where we'd played handball, and through the Village all the way up Broadway to the block where Walter lived. I stood looking up at Badmouth's red light glowing in the window. I remembered when Walter told me that snakes don't see red.

By the time I got home I knew how I'd paint the chameleon. I tiptoed to my room, went up the ladder, and turned on the light beside my bed. Sitting cross-legged I spread out the jacket. I couldn't draw the way Walter and I were holding the chameleon—I couldn't draw human hands—but it was okay, because Walter would know the chameleon and remember. So I drew a branch going diagonally across the front of the jacket. I drew the chameleon climbing up the branch, holding on to the base with the tip of her tail. Her mitten hand reached out, almost grasping the upper part of the branch.

I used all the greens in my paint box to get the chameleon right. A drop of gold and a smaller spot of black in the middle for her eye and she was done. Carefully I moved the jacket from my bed, turned off the light, and put my head down on the pillow. I wondered what Walter was doing in California. What was his mother like? Was he surfing, or playing volleyball on the beach with a bunch of girls? I pulled the sheet over my head and tried to think about something else, but my mind kept going back there. Finally I fell asleep.

When the first light came into my room I reached over and touched the chameleon—the paint was dry. A wave of nerves in my stomach woke me up all the way. Even though Walter wouldn't be there, nothing was stopping me from taking the jacket to Fang & Claw so that he'd find it waiting there Monday. I folded the jacket and wrapped it up in a big plastic bag and left before my mother was up.

On Sundays the trains were always slow. I waited on the platform in the empty station, hearing the distant rumble of a train somewhere in the tunnel and feeling the coolness of the underground air and the current of nervous excitement that passed through me.

The morning sunshine made the Fang & Claw sign extra-white and the details of the storefront look crisp. The criss-crossed iron gate with its oiled joints and the steel padlock with rusty flecks were lit up, and the black window was more like a mirror than ever. I saw me in my Bronx Zoo Reptile House T-shirt. It was nice not to see a glowering face looking back.

Inside, the pale violet lights were on. The turtles would be up basking on their rocks, each with a back leg sticking out. Some of the frogs would be waking up, while others slept in the high corners of their tanks. Sue was coiled around her eggs. I thought about the spider in the jar with her legs drawn in tight, all cocooned inside her own silk. I thought about how terrible it was that no one could touch her.

Squatting at the gate, I pushed the bag with the jacket inside between the bars, careful not to tear the plastic. It fell through and landed with a plop. I put my arm through as far as it would go, almost to my elbow, and gave the package a good shove so it was up against the door, out of reach. Then I realized that someone could get it with an umbrella or a broomstick or something. I looked around and couldn't see anything I could use to get it back, but neither could I see anyone watching, or even anyone nearby who might have seen. I had to hope that no one would bother with a thing wrapped in an old plastic bag.

Tomorrow school would start again, and afterward I'd come see if Walter liked the jacket. I stood up and brushed off my hands on my jeans and started walking home.

People were beginning to come out to get thick Sunday newspapers and paper bags of bagels or croissants. Smells of coffee and baked things wafted out of cafés and bakeries that had their doors open. I stopped and bought some fresh pastries to have at home with my mother. I bought blueberries for the lizards at the green market.

My favorite thing to do was read in the lizard room. Sunday afternoon I sat in a chair with my feet up on the windowsill, reading my science fiction novel. Spot had come down and was making a racket on the cage wire with his claws. He'd climbed up in my lap and then stretched himself out across my legs and bobbed his big head up and down. Jane looked down at him agreeably. When the phone rang I realized I'd forgotten to call Cathy. I put Spot on my shoulder and hurried to answer.

"Hello?" said the voice.

My insides felt like a feather pillow bursting. "Walter."

"Grace, your jacket—it was in the doorway and I can't figure—well, are you—did you—"

"It's for you."

"Really?"

"Yes—I've been working with Pops all week and we—I missed you."

"You did? Do you want to come see the pictures I took in California? I went hiking every day in the canyons and you wouldn't believe all the herps out there. I got a great shot of a Pacific Coast rattler, and one of a fence swift sitting right on top of an old fencepost, just like a postcard. And there are tarantulas out there like crazy, and I caught the best-looking Cal king I ever saw." He paused. "So, are you coming?"

"Where are you?"

"Home. I went to the shop to check on Sue, but now I'm here."

"Be there as soon as I can."

Hugging and kissing Spot, I hurried back to his room and set him beside Jane. I brushed my hair, grabbed my keys, and went out the door.

Walter was wearing the jacket when he opened the door.

"It fits you better than it fit me."

"I love it."

We sat cross-legged on the floor in Walter's room and looked at pictures of canyons and snakes and lizards. Badmouth circled us, tongue flicking.

"He's still restless," I said. "So I was hoping you'd think about taking Python. I've got the iguanas, and you know how that is. I don't want you to think I'm trying to get rid of her, though, because I'll keep her before I'll let anyone else have her."

"Actually, I thought about it a long time ago, but she's your snake, so I didn't mention it. I'd love to have Python. She's a survivor and a perfect match for Badmouth."

"Do you think they'll like each other?"

"Oh, they will. I know how to play with light and temperature and humidity to put them in the mood." Walter reached out and rested his hand on Badmouth. "Hey, I nearly forgot—I brought something back for you."

Searching through the suitcase he hadn't unpacked, Walter pulled out a T-shirt and held it up. SOUTHWESTERN HERPETOLOGICAL SOCIETY was printed on the front in blue letters, with a collared lizard underneath.

"I went to a meeting one night and bought us each one."

I took the shirt from Walter and put it right on over my Bronx Zoo shirt, and he laughed.

"It's so funny," I said. "I was sure you were on the beach, surfing or something."

"Me? I turn pink under a lightbulb."

I looked down at my hand where the rock python had bitten me, and I spread my fingers to see the little white scars. "Oh, Walter, I'm so sorry about what I said. I didn't mean it—I love the way you look. It was me I hated. And when you tried to kiss my hand? I couldn't understand that at all, because why would you want to do that, when I'm so disgusting?"

"But you're not—why do you say that?"

Walter's eyes were as still and gray as Badmouth's. I reached for him and gave him the biggest python hug ever.

ACKNOWLEDGMENTS

Fang & Claw was a real place. I am grateful to the proprietor for permission to use the name.

Thank you, Helen Robinson and Katya Rice. I am so moved by how deeply you read this story and by what you have given to it.

And to Mark Keoppen, Diane Townsend, Judah Catalan, Nobuko Meaders, Jack Ludwig, Zeb Schachtel, Steve Lewis, Jane Resh Thomas, Phyllis Root, Carolyn Coman, Norma Fox Mazer, and Stephen Roxburgh—what feelings I have for each of you! I should find my own words, but these words of Muriel Rukeyser's say it best: "There are so many ways in which one is conducted to learning, so many ways in which one seeks, and ways in which one loves the people from whom one can learn."